CAMP MUSKY

CAMP MUSKY

David DeLong

Kravitz & Sons
INNOVATORS IN PUBLISHING, MARKETING AND ADVERTISING

Kravitz and Sons LLC
1301 Farmville Blvd, Suite 104
Greenville, NC 27834

Published by Kravitz and Sons LLC.

ISBN: 979-8-89639-082-4 (sc)
ISBN: 979-8-89639-081-7 (e)

Library of Congress Control Number: 2025902700

Because of the dynamic nature of the Internet, any web addresses or links contained in this book may have changed since publication and may no longer be valid. The views expressed in this work are solely those of the author and do not necessarily reflect the views of the publisher, and the publisher hereby disclaims any responsibility for them.

TABLE OF CONTENTS

CHAPTER 1

The sport-utility vehicle bounced along the gravel road as clouds of dust billowed up from under and behind it. The vehicle had just turned off from the main road—Highway 27—which led to a town called Moose Lake. It was now on an unpaved lane, which the sign at the intersection had indicated, went to a recreation site called Camp Musky.

Buddy and Cally Chambers, the two sibling occupants seated in the middle section of the SUV, were about to burst with excitement at the thought of spending one full week away from home at summer church camp. Buddy had been here last year, but this was Cally's first time at camp.

"Look!" Cally exclaimed, pointing her extended index finger. "There's the big musky sign out in front of the camp!"

The sign, which was in the shape of a big musky fish, was barely visible through the dust that Dad had to clear from the SUVs windshield by using the wipers.

Cally, who was twelve years old, loved to tease her year-older brother, and now she found an opportunity to do just that.

"Ha! ha! I saw the sign first," she quipped. Her lips parted in a self-satisfied smile.

"Big deal!" Buddy snapped as his eyes left the musky sign and looked out a side window to a chipmunk that was sitting on a stump. He loved his younger sister, but sometimes her teasing got to him a little bit.

"Well, we're almost there." Mom interrupted the teasing session as she glanced from Cally to Buddy, and back to Cally with a faint smile on her face. She knew that the teasing could get out of hand quickly.

The SUV pulled up to a log building that read "Registration" above its door, and Dad said, "Okay! That's the end of the line!" He turned the key off, and the motor died.

The four climbed out of the SUV and entered the registration room which had mounted deer and moose heads on the walls. There was already a line of people ahead of them waiting to be registered for camp. A large boy with thick glasses, who was about Buddy's age, was just ahead of them standing in the line with a man whom the Chambers assumed was his dad. The boy turned around and bug-eyed Buddy and Cally for several moments.

Buddy spoke first. "Hi, I'm Buddy Chambers, and this is my sister, Cally. What's your name?"

The boy crinkled up his nose, his eyes looking big behind the thick lenses, and stared suspiciously at the pair. When he didn't answer right away, the man standing next to him poked him slightly with his elbow. "Answer them, Stanley."

The boy's face reddened a bit. "I'm...I'm Stanley Foster," he stammered.

"Looks like we'll be seeing quite a bit of each other the next few days, Stanley," Buddy said to him with a smile.

Stanley just shrugged.

"By the way, why do they call this place Camp Musky?" Cally asked innocently.

Stanley's big eyes got even bigger behind his glasses. "You mean you don't know?"

"Don't know what?" Cally's eyes were now starting to get big.

"They call this place Camp Musky because of the huge muskellunge fish that swims out there in the lake!" Stanley pointed toward the lake a few hundred yards from the building they were in called Moose Lake from which the town, about ten miles away, received its name.

Buddy and Cally looked with a feeling of wonder through a window of the building toward the lake to which Stanley had pointed.

"How big is this fish supposed to be?" Buddy asked with great interest.

"Oh, I'd say about ten or twelve feet long, and it weighs maybe five hundred pounds," Stanley said slowly and deliberately for the effect it would have on the Chambers kids.

"Stanley, stop your fibbing," the man beside him commanded. "You know very well that that musky in Moose Lake is only about six feet long and weighs possibly something over one hundred pounds. At least that's what some fishermen have said who have hooked the monster!"

"That's still a really big fish!" Mr. Chambers said, breaking into the conversation. "I've never heard of a musky getting that big. I believe the world record is only about sixty-seven pounds or so."

"Hi, my name is Peter Foster," the man next to Stanley said as he shook hands with Mr. and Mrs. Chambers. "Well, that's how big the eyewitnesses have said the fish apparently is anyway," he added.

"I thought this place was called Camp Musky because of the large amounts of musky fish caught in the lake," Buddy said as he looked into his dad's face.

"That's what I thought too," Mr. Chambers said, raising his eyebrows. "But maybe we were wrong."

Stanley was enjoying his celebrity status as the one who had introduced the subject of the big fish. He was enjoying too the reaction of fear that was expressed upon Cally's face to the news of this monster in Moose Lake. And most of all, he was enjoying his acquaintance with the girl herself. She was actually quite pretty, Stanley thought with her auburn hair, green eyes, and slightly upturned nose. But he wasn't about to give her the satisfaction of telling her these thoughts. No sir, not Stanley Foster!

"I've heard that some folks have been attacked by the musky while swimming in Moose Lake," Stanley said nonchalantly, looking for a reaction from Cally.

"What do you mean attacked?" Cally asked with a shiver running down her spine.

Stanley noticed her reaction with pleasure. "Well, I've heard that some folks were bitten by the musky while swimming. I guess it was kind of like a shark attack only with a musky. They say that some of the bites were quite serious too."

By now, the line had worked its way up to Stanley and his dad, who had to turn from their conversation with the Chambers so that Stanley could get registered for camp. After being registered and as Stanley was walking away, he said to Cally, "See you and Buddy this afternoon in the Moose Lake at swimming time!"

Cally stared at him with a look of shock on her face. Stanley grinned back at her with obvious satisfaction.

The Chambers came up to the registration desk. The man who was doing the registering was surprisingly young, probably in his early twenties. But he was also kind of cute, Cally thought.

"Hello, folks!" the young man said. "My name is Randy Brewer. I'm the Youth Pastor at one of the local denominations, and I'm in charge of camp for the next week or so." He shook hands with Mr. and Mrs. Chambers.

Buddy and Cally were introduced to Pastor Randy, and then they were registered, each being assigned to a cabin. Buddy's cabin was number three in the boys' section, of course. And Cally's cabin was number seven in the girls' section.

A little later, the Chambers kids got settled into their respective cabins, and Mom and Dad said their goodbyes with a few final instructions.

"Make sure you write us a couple of times," Mom said with a tear trickling down her face. "We love you both. Take good care of yourselves. Buddy, I want you to look after your sister, okay?"

Buddy promised that he would. And after they all had a time of hugs and kisses and a prayer, Mom and Dad Chambers returned home.

* * * * *

The time taken for registration, the settling of the kids into their cabins, and the farewells had taken the Chambers about two hours. Therefore, it was now about 3:00 p.m., the beginning of swim time in Moose Lake. Because of supervision conflicts, all scheduled activities were mandatory so that no camper was allowed to be on his or her own. So, Buddy and Cally changed into their swimsuits and headed down to the lake. They met on the trail that led to that body of water.

"Do you think that we could be attacked by the big musky while we're swimming?" Cally asked her brother anxiously.

"I doubt it," Buddy replied, trying to sound like he was courageous. "We don't even know if such a fish really exists. I mean, come on, we only have Stanley and his dad's word for it. And they've never seen the fish personally. Everything they know about it has come from reports by other people. It could all just be a big hoax to try to scare people."

Cally wasn't reassured by her brother's comments. But since she wasn't sure she would actually get into the water to swim anyway, she dismissed her thoughts about the monster fish.

Soon the two were at Moose Lake. They noticed that Stanley and a group of other kids were already in the water. One of the boys was dunking some of the swimmers' heads underwater until a shrill whistle and a shouted command from the lifeguard told him to stop.

Stanley noticed the Chambers kids at the water's edge. "Come on in, you two! The water is great!"

Buddy waded in up to his waist, and then plunged into the gray-green waters of the lake. He surfaced a short distance away and started doing a backstroke.

Cally only went in ankle deep. A shiver ran down her spine for a second time. She wasn't sure if it was from the water, which felt a tad bit cool, or from a subconscious reaction relating to the musky stories.

Stanley noticed her hesitation and smiled to himself. He loved it! "Come on in, Cally coward," he teased. "No big musky has bitten me yet. I dare you to dive right in! No, I double-dog dare you!" Stanley looked around at the other swimmers who had stopped long enough to see what was going on between him and this newcomer to camp. Some of the other boys were now grinning and taking up the dare with Cally.

She waded in a little deeper. Now she was up to her knees in the sand-stirred water. She was about to take another step, when suddenly she felt something nip her on the leg. Cally shrieked and jumped straight up. Then she dashed for the shore.

Stanley and some of the others laughed hilariously. Finally, he said, "Oh brother! Cally, that was probably just a little bluegill that nipped one of your unshaven leg hairs! They do it to me all the time." Stanley was still enjoying the whole situation with Cally, giving high fives to his friends, and chuckling over her fright, when suddenly he felt sharp teeth biting into one of his legs. He screamed from pain and fright and made a frenzied beeline dash for the shore. "It bit me!" he shouted. "The monster musky just bit me on the leg!"

Just then, Buddy broke the surface of the water with a big grin upon his face. "Boy, Foster, you taste a little salty," he razzed, spitting make-believe pieces of flesh from his mouth.

Stanley stared at him for a moment in disbelief. Then he yelled, "I'm going to punch your face in, Chambers!"

By now, everyone at the lake—the lifeguard included—was laughing so hard they could hardly stand or sit up.

Stanley splashed his way out of the lake, glaring at Cally as he went by. She turned her head and snickered, her hand covering her mouth. Stanley stomped directly to his cabin even though he knew he wasn't supposed to be there now.

Nearly all the campers present congratulated Buddy at his cleverness, wishing they had thought of the trick first.

Buddy came over to his sister who was still smiling broadly.

"That was a good one, Buddy!" she said, admiring him for sticking up for her.

Buddy shrugged. "Yeah, I guess so, Sis. I do feel kind of bad for Stanley though. The way I humiliated him in front of everybody."

"But he was trying to humiliate me in front of everybody," she replied.

"I know. But two wrongs don't make a right, Cal. I've probably just made an enemy."

"Are you going to apologize to him?" Cally asked, touching her brother on his arm.

"I don't know. Maybe I should."

At that moment, Pastor Randy came up to the pair. "Hi, guys. Are you having a good time?"

They both nodded their agreement.

"I thought I'd get a little swim time in before supper."

Cally's heart fluttered a bit as she watched him go into the water. Soon she was back in the lake by herself, having forgotten all about the big musky stories, and the incident with Stanley.

Buddy sat on one of the available benches and became preoccupied in his thoughts for the remainder of the swimming session.

At 5:00 p.m., the lifeguard blew her whistle, signaling everyone that the lake was now officially closed. She also announced that supper would be at five-thirty in the cafeteria, and that everyone needed to be dressed in their regular clothes for that event.

Buddy and Cally each went to their respective cabins, changed their clothes, and then met up in the cafeteria.

"Did you see Stanley?" Cally asked.

"No. He is registered in a different cabin from mine," Buddy said. "But speaking of the devil, there he comes through the cafeteria door."

Cally looked up as Stanley came into the cafeteria and plunked himself down at the nearest table. He still looked pretty "ticked off."

"Here goes," Buddy said as he headed in Stanley's direction. Reaching the dreaded table, Buddy spoke apologetically. "Stanley, I'm sorry for biting you on the leg and doing it in front of everyone out at the lake."

Stanley's eyes blazed at Buddy as he exclaimed, "Tell it to somebody who cares, Chambers! You've still got a good beating coming from me! I always get even! And I pick the time and place when it happens!"

Buddy, realizing that any further conversation with Stanley would do no good, turned and walked back to his sister. "Well, Sis, I sure enough did make an enemy of Stanley!"

"But I'm still glad you defended my honor out at the lake, Buddy."

They picked a table and sat down. Buddy purposely sat with his back to Stanley, so he wouldn't "accidentally" have eye contact with him.

Pastor Randy came into the room and announced that he would be dismissing tables after the blessing was said on the meal. The campers then were to line up and get their meals cafeteria style.

Pastor Randy had all the campers bow their heads while he asked the blessing and gave the Lord thanks for the food. Then wouldn't you know it? He dismissed old Stanley's table first.

Stanley pushed his way to the front of the line, elbowing a couple of kids who were smaller than he was.

"Foster, no shoving your way in line!" Pastor Randy commanded. "Just for that, you go to the back of the line!"

Stanley, who already was in a foul mood, stomped his way to the back of his group's line.

"Serves him right," Buddy whispered to Cally with a slight grin on his face.

The tables that the campers were seated at were really picnic tables covered with tablecloths. The seats, though, were separate benches to the tables. When Stanley came by the Chambers' table, following his line to get supper, he purposely tripped over their bench, making it look like an accident. The bench upset, and everyone on it toppled to the floor. Buddy and Cally sprawled over each other, and Cally whacked her head pretty hard on the floor.

"Ow!" she cried, holding the side of her head.

"Oh, I'm so sorry," Stanley said with a mock apology. "Did you get hurt, Cally?"

"You did it on purpose, Foster!" Buddy accused him.

Pastor Randy came quickly over to the scene. "What happened here?"

"Oh, I'm just a bit clumsy tonight," Stanley said with a sheepish smile. "I'm sorry, everyone!"

"Just get your food, Foster," Pastor Randy ordered. Then he gave his attention to Cally. "Are you all right, honey?" He helped her up from the floor.

Cally rubbed her head a little, then smiled at the youth pastor. "I am now!"

Everyone in the cafeteria let out a collective, "Ohhh!"

Cally, a little red-faced, sat back on the bench with the others who had fallen off.

Pastor Randy dismissed the Chambers' table next. They all picked their choices from a variety of food including mashed potatoes and gravy, corn on the cob, salad, rolls with butter and jelly, several other vegetables, and a good assortment of desserts and drinks. It seemed to everyone who had any camp experience that the best menu was served the first night. After that, the food variety quickly diminished, the longer that camp went on. It probably had something to do with the budget. Anyway, one might as well feast when one had the opportunity to do so.

No sooner had the folks at the Chambers' table been seated again when—slop! A gob of gooey mashed potatoes landed on the back of Buddy's head. He reached up and smeared it off his hair, then looked around to the only person he knew would have done it.

"All right, Foster! Quit slingin' potatoes at me!"

Stanley had his head down and was eating his food slowly, pretending to mind his own business. "I didn't sling potatoes at you," he said, looking very innocent.

Pastor Randy said forcefully, "There will be no food fights in this cafeteria! Is that understood?"

Everyone nodded their heads affirmatively.

"Now," the youth pastor continued. "Did anyone see who slung potatoes at Buddy?"

Nobody said a word. The silence was so obvious that the clock ticking on the wall could be heard.

"If I catch anyone throwing food for any reason," Pastor Randy said, "I will personally give him or her extra chores to do as a punishment!"

A couple of boys at Stanley's table snickered.

Pastor Randy eyed them but held his tongue. "Now then, after supper is over, you will have about an hour before we go to the campfire service at seven-thirty. The service there will last to about nine-thirty. So, you can go back to your cabins and rest up a bit, or you can visit with your friends. Just be sure to meet in front of the cafeteria before seven-thirty. Oh, and bring your flashlights and bug spray. This would also be a good time to learn the camp rules and schedule that I'm going to pass out to you in a moment. We've already sent a copy of these rules and schedule to your homes last week, so maybe you are familiar with these rules. Any questions?"

There weren't any, so Pastor Randy finished dismissing the tables, and he also handed out to each camper a sheet of paper that contained a list of the rules and the schedule for this year's camp.

Buddy and Cally read the list while they ate.

Schedule

7:00 a.m.	Wake-up time
7:30 a.m.	Morning devotions
8:00 a.m.	Breakfast
8:30 a.m.- noon	Classes
12:30 p.m.	Lunch
1:30 p.m.-3:00 p.m.	Outdoor activities
3:00 p.m.-5:00 p.m.	Swim time
5:30 p.m.	Supper
6:30 p.m.-7:30 p.m.	Free time
7:30 p.m.-9:30 p.m.	Campfire service
10:00 p.m.	Bedtime, lights out!

What not to bring to camp: drugs, tobacco, alcohol, matches, guns, knives with blades longer than three inches, fireworks, magazines, radios, CD players, and bad attitudes.

What to bring to camp: Bibles, appropriate camp clothing, swimsuits, money for snacks, flashlights, bug spray, notebooks and pens/pencils, smiles, and good attitudes.

Responsibilities: Each camper will be assigned to a cabin. The whole cabin as a unit will perform various chores as listed in the camp directory on specified days. There will be no fighting or roughhousing at camp. There will be no food fights in the cafeteria. Appropriate clothing is to be worn at all times. Campers must be accounted for at all times. Strict adherence to the schedule must be followed. Above all, respect God, other campers, and the possessions of others. Violation of these rules will result in various punishments, up to and including, expulsion from camp. Now, have fun!

Buddy folded the sheet of paper and put it in his shirt pocket. "There's nothing in the rules or schedule that I can't handle, especially since I already knew of some of the rules from last year."

Cally nodded. "Yeah, it was also a good thing that the camp mailed out to us the camp's requirements about a week before we got here. At least among other things, I knew to bring a flashlight and bug spray. The mosquitos get really bad after dark."

"Well, I hope the human bugs don't get really bad after dark," replied Buddy, glancing over at Stanley.

Cally grinned. "I know what you mean, bro."

The Chambers kids visited for a while with some of the other campers, then each went back to his or her cabin to get ready for the campfire service.

A little before seven-thirty, the campers met in front of the cafeteria as Pastor Randy had told them to. As usual, some of the campers had neglected to bring mosquito spray, and now they were begging some of the "responsible" campers for a night's dose of this "relief juice," especially as the blood-sucking insects were now out in full force.

Soon Pastor Randy joined the kids and hushed their conversation with a loud, "Listen up, guys! I've just learned this evening that a couple of senior pastors from the denomination will be at the campfire service tonight. They're here to evaluate me so please, please be on your best behavior! Okay?"

Stanley rather loudly whispered to one of his friends, "Oh, so he wants to impress his superiors!" They both giggled.

"What was that, Foster?" asked Pastor Randy with an obvious frown on his face.

"Oh, nothing, sir!" replied Stanley, contorting his face to keep from smiling.

Pastor Randy cleared his throat. "All right then. Let's go to the campfire!" He led the way. His turned-off flashlight swung rapidly back and forth in his right hand as he strode confidently up the trail to meet with the senior pastors at the campfire area. He was determined to meet their expectations! He would perform well for them! He most assuredly would impress them! Pastor Randy winced at that last thought. That's what he thought he'd heard Stanley Foster say about him. Well anyway, he had to try to do his best. They were out here to grade his performance.

He slowed his gait somewhat and allowed the flashlight to come to a rest by his side. He didn't need the light yet because at this time of the year in the north country, the sun wouldn't set for another hour or so anyway.

He looked behind him, noticing that some of the campers were breathing hard, and beginning to perspire. The last one coming was Stanley, who seemed to be having an especially hard time keeping up with the rest. Pastor Randy let them all catch up together and allowed them to rest a while.

Stanley, who was a little humiliated at being the last one to catch up stayed, as well as he could by the youth pastor's side when they started up again. So did Buddy and Cally.

Rounding a bend in the trail, the little group noticed an old mansion-style house several hundred yards away, covered with ivy vines, and looking very mysterious.

"What is that spooky-looking place?" Cally asked with a tone of wonder in her voice.

"Oh, that mansion is the home of Horace and Hector Chillblaines, two eccentric millionaire bachelor brothers who don't get out much it seems, and who would like to see Camp Musky closed down," replied Pastor Randy with a frown.

"Closed down!" exclaimed Buddy. "But why?"

"Well for one thing apparently, they don't like the noise that the campers who come here make. Or something like that. I'm not really sure," Pastor Randy replied.

They all including Stanley watched the big house with fascination until another bend in the trail blocked it from their sight.

Buddy had more questions about the Chillblaines, but the group was now near the campfire site, so he refrained from asking them.

A fairly large bonfire was blazing in the center of a clearing in the forest. Well away from the fire and set back toward the outer ring of trees in the clearing, were log benches on which the campers sat. These benches began filling up as the group filed into the clearing, and the campers took their seats around the fire. Seated conspicuously by themselves were the two senior pastors who Pastor Randy had said would be there. Buddy thought they looked awfully serious for a campfire service, when such a service usually meant high-spirited singing, hand clapping, and a generally all-around good time.

Pastor Randy clapped his hands together and called for the excited campers to settle down. "All right, everyone!" he exclaimed with a tone of great authority. "I'd like to introduce to you Pastor

Brown and Pastor Baxter, who are here this evening to watch, I mean fellowship with us."

The two senior pastors nodded their acknowledgment of the group. "Okay, then," Pastor Randy continued, "let's begin our campfire service by singing some choruses."

The group heartily sang some of their favorite choruses such as "Jesus Is the Sweetest Name I Know," "Every Day with Jesus Is Sweeter Than the Day Before," and "Come into My Heart, Lord Jesus." After about twenty minutes of singing, Pastor Randy said a prayer and then began his campfire devotional talk.

The topic of his talk this evening was the Bible story of the three young men in the fiery furnace from the book of Daniel chapter 3. Pastor Randy gave a really inspiring talk of how these three youths trusted completely in God even though they were thrown into a furnace of fire because they refused to bow down to an idol. He even gave his words more emphasis by tossing three sticks into the campfire. Every eye followed those sticks as they landed in the center of the blaze. Pastor Randy finished the gripping story by saying that God saved those three youths from being harmed in the furnace, and that God will still help young people today who put their trust in Him. When he finished, every head was bowed in thought about what he had just said.

Pastor Randy looked around the circle of campers, realizing that not a word was being spoken, not even by Stanley Foster. He fully believed in the Bible including the story he had just told. But just now, a little pride was swelling up in his heart and mind. *"Wow!"* he thought. *"I've really made quite an impression on the kids tonight!"* He glanced up at the senior pastors who were now looking at him with smiles upon their faces. *"Man, oh man,"* he mused. *"I've made a great impression on my superiors too!"*

For several moments now, he had been standing motionless, a little too close to the campfire while relishing these very pleasant thoughts. He didn't realize that his pant legs had become quite hot until he stepped forward, and his pants came in contact with the skin of his legs. Pastor Randy jumped up and down, contorting his body in wild gestures and letting out earpiercing whoops.

Both of the senior pastors stared in disbelief at him.

Pastor Brown looked over at Pastor Baxter and said rather dryly, "I didn't know that our brother in the faith had taken up worldly dancing. We can't have that! I'm afraid this won't look good on his report! No, sir, not at all!"

Pastor Baxter nodded solemnly then repeated, "No, sir, not at all!"

Pastor Randy by now had recovered from his pain and was looking sheepishly as the campers continued to laugh hysterically at his antics, and the two senior pastors shook their heads at him.

Then as Pastor Randy tried to forget his humiliation for the next hour or so, everyone toasted marshmallows on sticks and drank sodas from cans while the campfire crackled and sent showers of red sparks into the air. What glorious memories were being made tonight that would last a lifetime.

Finally, the joyous festivities for the evening came to an end when Pastor Randy said it was time for everybody to go back to their cabins and get some sleep. So, they put out the campfire and got their gear. Then following the youth pastor, the group headed back down the trail to go to their respective cabins.

On the way back, Buddy and Cally noticed that the lights were on in the spooky-looking mansion.

* * * * *

In that old vine-covered mansion, Horace Chillblaines was standing by one of the upstairs windows, his crooked hand still holding on to the drawn back curtain as he peered out at the campers who were making their way to their cabins by flashlight. He spoke in a wizened voice to his brother Hector, who was standing just behind him and who was also intently peering out the window at the campers. "We've got to stop those brats from spoiling our peace and quiet, you know, don't you, Hector? This happens every year, and I can't stand it anymore!"

"Yes," replied his brother with a sneer. "This is the year that we put a stop to it!"

* * * * *

Later that evening as everyone was sound asleep, the moon arose over the region full and bright. A large muskrat swam in the calm waters of Moose Lake when suddenly the surface of the lake erupted in a burst of spray that looked like thousands of crimson diamonds in the moonlight. Just as suddenly, the muskrat was gone.

Chapter 2

Pastor Randy was up at seven the next morning. After showering and dressing, he left his cabin number one, which was reserved for him as head counsellor, and entered the fresh air of a gorgeous summer morning. Since he had a few minutes before devotion time, he headed down to the edge of Moose Lake to take in the beauty and peace of the scene before him and to reflect upon what had happened at the campfire scene last evening.

"I guess I made an idiot out of myself and right in front of Pastors Brown and Baxter. Well, I probably was being humbled for my pride and for trying to impress my superiors. Anyway at least that experience is over even if they give me a poor rating on my performance. And furthermore, that was the only time they will be here during this year's camp. So, I can relax now and just be myself."

He was musing upon these thoughts when he happened to glance down at the mud along the shoreline of the lake. "What in the world?" he spoke out loud as he noticed huge tracks embedded in the mud. They seemed to be coming from and going back to the forest several hundred feet away. They resembled human footprints only they were much larger, about sixteen inches long and six inches wide. He thought they might be bear tracks as bears were the largest creatures that he knew of in the area. But the tracks actually looked more like some samples he had seen in a book on the wilds of the north country. "No, they can't belong to a legendary beast known as Bigfoot, can they? Surely such an animal doesn't even exist!" A shudder ran up his spine.

Well, anyway, it was just about time for devotions, so Pastor Randy headed for the cafeteria where the other campers were supposed to be assembled. He reached the cafeteria right at seven-thirty and then led the group in singing choruses for about five minutes. He prayed for everyone's safety for today and asked the Lord's blessing upon the food. Then he dismissed the campers to eat breakfast.

As they were eating, he announced that he had important business to discuss with them this morning. "I believe it is best for me to get straight to the point," he said, shifting from one foot to another. "This may well be the last year for Camp Musky to be open."

"Why?" came the surprised and frustrated question of almost every camper in the cafeteria.

Pastor Randy surveyed the room with a lump in his throat. For a moment, he couldn't speak. He had known many of these youngsters from camps before. Others were from his church group back home. But in every case, he felt an intense love for each one including those he was only beginning to know at this year's camp.

"Well," he began. His eyes got misty. "As some of you may or may not know, Horace and Hector Chillblaines, the two brothers who live in that ivy-covered mansion over there near the campfire site, have made a twenty-year lease with Camp Musky. That means that they have been letting us use their land for camping purposes these past twenty years, but this year is the last of the twenty years, and the lease will then run out. We have recently gotten a letter from the Chillblaines stating that they will not renew the lease after this year. So then, the camp will probably have to close if that is the case."

"You mean that Camp Musky is owned by the Chillblaines?" Buddy asked in surprise.

"Camp Musky owns the buildings but not the lake or the land," Pastor Randy replied. "You see, twenty years ago the Chillblaines allowed Camp Musky to be built on their own property, and then leased out the property for twenty years to any church group who wanted to use it. We're not the only group to use the facilities. Other churches have camps here throughout the year. The thing that puzzles me now is why the Chillblaines won't renew the lease. Without the use of their land, the buildings really can't be used either. Something must have really upset the Chillblaines."

"You said last evening that the Chillblaines didn't like the campers making noise, didn't you Pastor Randy?" Buddy asked.

"Yes, but that doesn't seem to me to be the real reason they won't renew the lease," Pastor Randy said thoughtfully. "I can't help but think that something else has caused them to make that decision. But whatever the reason is, the bottom line is that we may not have camp here next year, and that just about breaks my heart!"

Everyone sat in silence for some time. Finally, Pastor Randy said that they should pray about the situation, which they did. Then he said, "Okay, everybody, it's just about time for classes to begin. But before we dismiss, I have just one more announcement to make. I think there might be a bear that's been coming around the camp. I've just seen some large tracks down by the lakeshore this morning. So please be careful! That's all. You're dismissed to classes."

Buddy and Cally glanced at one another in astonishment but didn't say anything.

Stanley, however, spoke loudly so all the campers could hear, "I wouldn't be surprised if we had a killer grizzly bear on the campgrounds. Or maybe even a giant Bigfoot. These animals have been known to attack cabins at night! They make awful screeching noises, and they have a terrible stink about them." He looked about the group, watching for the usual reactions of fear that would come from such an announcement.

"Foster, shut your mouth and get to class!" Pastor Randy commanded. "The tracks most likely are from a black bear which is probably more afraid of us than the other way around. All I'm saying is that you should be careful and don't try to provoke the creature if you do happen to see one."

Stanley snickered and then left with the other campers to go to their respective classes.

Cally's first class was a quilting class. She wanted to make a pair of quilted hot pads for her mom. Buddy went to the woodworking class, where he hoped to make a wooden lampstand for his dad this week.

The second class for both siblings was Bible class. The Chambers kids sat side-by-side and were chatting before the class began. Stanley Foster, of all people came up and sat behind Cally. He tugged her braids and made her say, "Ow!"

Then Stanley looked at Buddy and made a face at him.

"Let's settle down, everyone! Class is about to begin!" Pastor Randy had just entered the room and had set his briefcase on the table in front of him. "This Bible class, which will be for the duration of camp, is on the "Life of Jesus," he continued, writing that heading on a blackboard. "Now then, can anyone tell me what is so important about Jesus?"

A girl, about Cally's age, raised her hand, and when asked to respond, she said, "Jesus is the Son of God and was born of the Virgin Mary."

"Very good!" Pastor Randy exclaimed. He began to discuss these facts with the rest of the class.

Meanwhile, Stanley muttered loud enough for Buddy and Cally to hear, "How can a woman have a child when she's a virgin?"

Cally whispered immediately to him. "God is Jesus's Father not Joseph. God performed a miracle upon Mary and conceived Jesus in her womb."

"How come you're so smart?" Stanley demanded of Cally with a sneer.

"Because I read my Bible and listen to my pastor preach in church," Cally replied matter-of-factly. "Don't you read the Bible, Stanley?"

Stanley hesitated some before answering. "My parents gave me a Bible some years ago, but I don't read it. Anyway, it reminds me of my mom every time I see it," he said, dropping his gaze to the floor.

"Did something happen to your mom?" Buddy inquired delicately.

"I really don't want to talk to you, Chambers," Stanley hissed through his clenched teeth. "But if you must know, she passed away several years ago, and my grandma and great-aunt both passed away with her. It was a car wreck."

"Oh, I'm sorry, man," Buddy said.

Just then, Pastor Randy interrupted their conversation. "Stanley, Buddy, and Cally, do you guys have something you want to share with the class?"

The three shook their heads vigorously.

"Well then, maybe you should be paying more attention in class, okay?"

They agreed.

"Now then," Pastor Randy continued. "What else is important about Jesus?"

Buddy raised his hand and received recognition to answer the question. "Jesus died on the cross to pay for our sins so that we can have eternal life with Him someday."

"Excellent, Buddy," Pastor Randy exclaimed, rubbing his hands together. "And how does one receive eternal life from Jesus?"

A boy named Jim answered the question. "We receive eternal life by repenting of our sins, asking Jesus into our life as Lord and Savior, being baptized in Jesus's name, receiving the Holy Spirit, and living our life for Him."

"That's really good, Jim," Pastor Randy beamed. "But what do we get in our lives today when we accept Jesus as Lord and Savior?"

Cally answered that one. "We get Jesus to help us through our lives now. He will help us solve our problems and He will give us peace."

Everyone could tell that Pastor Randy was really pleased by the answers that were given to his questions. He asked several more questions, and pretty soon the Bible class's time for today was over.

All the campers then went to their respective third and final class for the day. When it was finished, the time was twelve noon, one-half hour before lunch. Most of the campers went back to their cabins to put up their books and classroom supplies, and then got ready to go to the cafeteria for lunch.

Stanley, however, and a newly-formed friend named Roger went directly to the cafeteria to see if they could pilfer some snacks before the other campers got there. Stanley was holding his wooden slingshot that he'd made in shop class when the two sneaked inside the door.

Both boys ducked behind a counter so the cooking staff couldn't see them. They cautiously reached their hands to the top of the counter and felt around for cookies or other goodies they might find there. Since they didn't feel any food, they slowly raised their heads until their eyes could see above the counter top.

Stanley noticed the cooking staff going about their usual chores. But then, a slight movement above them on the cafeteria wall caught his attention. A mouse was crawling along a small piece of trim molding, probably trying to do the same thing that Stanley and Roger were trying to do—attempting to get some food without getting caught.

A mischievous thought entered Stanley's mind. He grinned at Roger, who by this time had seen the mouse, and then he reached into his pocket for one of the acorns he had stuffed there earlier. He put the acorn on the leather patch on his slingshot then took quick aim and released it at the mouse. The acorn missed the mouse by several inches, but it hit the wall with such force that it ricocheted downward like an arrow, hitting Ms. Betsy Baker (one of the cooks) on the back of the head. The blow from the acorn knocked her false teeth into the pot of bean stew she was cooking.

"Who-who-who shot me in the head?" Betsy sputtered.

Stanley and Roger, who had quickly ducked back down behind the counter, crept on their hands and knees until they got to the door. Then turning the knob, they burst through the door and ran as hard as they could. They didn't stop until they reached the cabin number six. Then they flopped down on two of the beds and laughed until the tears came out of their eyes.

"Did-did-did ya see Ms. Betsy's teeth fall into the stewpot?" Stanley gasped between the lung full of air he was gulping down.

"Yeah." Roger too was gasping. "And we made it out of the cafeteria just by the skin of our teeth."

When the two boys heard the word "teeth" they broke out for some minutes into uncontrollable laughter.

After a while, the "joke" became less funny to the boys and hunger began to grumble in their stomachs.

Finally, Stanley spoke, "Hey, Roger, it must be time for lunch. Let's get some chow."

"What if someone saw us hit Ms. Betsy or saw us running out of the cafeteria? We'd be in big trouble!" Roger reasoned.

"No one saw us," Stanley insisted, trying to reassure himself as well as Roger. "If they had, somebody would have come to the cabin by now. Anyway, I don't want to stay in this cabin and starve to death! Besides, staying up here would only be a sign that we're guilty."

"I guess you're right," Roger slowly admitted. "But let's not tell anyone even our friends that we or rather you shot her with an acorn." That last thought made Roger feel a little better. It wasn't actually he who had hit Ms. Betsy with the acorn, but rather it was Stanley who had done it. Maybe he wouldn't be in any trouble anyway.

It was about twelve-thirty when the pair exited the cabin and made their way down the trail to the cafeteria. As they rounded the last bend in the trail, they saw an ambulance parked in front of the cafeteria, its lights still whirling, sending red streaks across the buildings and onto the crowd that was gathered there.

Stanley and Roger could hardly believe their eyes. "I wonder who got hurt?" Stanley exclaimed, walking a little faster toward the ambulance. Roger followed him step for step.

Dr. Jerry Ravenbush, the camp physician, was standing next to Ms. Betsy Baker, who was seated on a bench on the cafeteria's porch.

Stanley's face paled. Was it Ms. Betsy who had been injured when the nut hit her head? *"Surely,"* he thought, *"that acorn couldn't have hit her with that much force!"* He decided to question the doctor.

"Uh, Dr. Ravenbush," Stanley began, "who go hurt? Why is the ambulance here?"

"Oh, hi, Stanley," Dr. Ravenbush greeted the boy. "Apparently an acorn was thrown or shot by someone, hitting Ms. Betsy here in the head. The acorn didn't do any damage to her head thankfully, but the shock of her being hit that way made her faint. She seems to be all right, but we called the ambulance as a precaution. You know when someone faints there's always the possibility of them hitting the floor too hard with their head. That was our main concern. She has a good bump on her forehead, and she has a headache but that seems to be the extent of her injuries."

Stanley nodded. "Why do you think it was an acorn that hit her?"

Dr. Ravenbush stared at Stanley for a moment. "Well, Ms. Betsy believes it was a small object that hit her, and we found an acorn lying near her on the floor. So, we're guessing that that's what it was."

"Oh, so no one actually witnessed Ms. Betsy being struck in the head?" Roger said, entering into the conversation.

"No, no one witnessed her being hit," Dr. Ravenbush replied. He noticed Stanley and Roger eyeing each other rather nervously. "Do you boys know anything about what happened?"

"N-no!" Stanley lied.

"Well, if you find out anything about the incident, please let me or Pastor Randy know about it. Okay, boys?"

The two boys nodded simultaneously.

"If we do find out, who did it," Dr. Ravenbush added, "the least that will happen to that person or persons is expulsion from camp. There could even be prosecution by the law for assault."

As the boys walked away from the doctor, they no longer felt that Ms. Betsy's "encounter" with the acorn was a joke. But Stanley tried to ease his conscience by whispering to Roger, "Well at least Ms. Betsy wasn't hurt very badly. This whole thing will blow over pretty quickly as long as neither of us whispers a word about it! Remember Roger, Dr. Ravenbush said that the person or persons responsible would be punished. You're an accessory to the incident. Which means you could be punished too."

"Don't worry, man!" Roger replied with a frown. "I'm not breathing a word to anyone about it."

"Good!" Stanley said with a twisted smile upon his face.

Then the two boys entered the cafeteria for lunch.

* * * * *

The rest of the afternoon and evening were fairly uneventful as the campers went routinely about their various activities including swim time, supper, and the campfire service.

The campers, however, did notice again the eerie-looking mansion on their way back to their cabins. This gave Stanley the idea to "spook" some of the guys when they got back to cabin number six, which was, of course, his cabin.

"Hey, guys!" he announced when they were about ready for lights out. "I've got a story to tell you. A ghost story!"

The boys all gathered on or around Stanley's bunk in anticipation of hearing a really scary tale, one that would raise the "goose bumps" on the backs of their necks.

"Well, the story goes something like this," Stanley whispered. "They say it was a number of years ago that a girl was out swimming in Moose Lake on a dark and moonless night. She had been warned not to swim out there without a lifeguard, but she wouldn't listen and went and snuck out on the lake anyway. Well, something pulled her underwater. To this day, nobody knows what it was. But many suspect it was the giant musky!" Stanley grabbed the nearest boy's arm when he stated the word "musky," making the boy yell out and pull his arm back. "Anyway," Stanley continued with a big grin, "the girl drowned, and they found her body floating on the lake the next day. Some say that you can see her ghost walking on Moose Lake when the moon is out full and bright!"

Stanley glanced around the room at the boys' faces to see their reactions to his story. Most of them were staring back at him with large eyes. One of the boys, named Clarence, a small, skinny kid who was twelve but who looked like he was eight was so scared that his teeth were chattering. When Stanley snickered about this, the boy said he wasn't really scared but just cold. Stanley just kept snickering.

Just then another "brilliant" thought crossed Stanley's brain. "Hey, fellas, let's really give the girls a big scare, okay?"

The boys thought it was a great idea and asked Stanley what his plan of action was.

"Well remember that Pastor Randy saw some large tracks down by the lake?" Stanley asked. "Let's make the girls think there really is a Bigfoot in these woods. We can make some screeching sounds and pound on their cabin walls."

"Yeah, yeah, that's great!" The boys responded to Stanley's suggestion.

The boys made sure that the lights were out in their cabin to make Pastor Randy believe that they were all in bed, then they sneaked out the cabin door and headed for the farthest girls' cabin away from Pastor Randy. This cabin of course was number seven, which just happened to be Cally's cabin also.

A boy named Benny tripped over a log and fell into a patch of blackberries.

"Yeow!" he yelled as the brambles stuck him in the arms and legs.

"Shh!" Stanley commanded through his clenched teeth.

Benny, whimpering, pulled himself out of the blackberry patch and picked the stickers out of his skin.

The boys then encircled cabin number seven, waiting for a signal from Stanley before "attacking" it.

The signal came from a high-sounding screech that Stanley manufactured by tightening up his vocal cords and forcing air through them at the same time.

The boys rushed up to the cabin from all sides and pounded on the log walls with their fists while they screeched, grunted, and snarled randomly.

Inside cabin number seven, the girls screamed.

Cally, though trembling some from the initial fright that they experienced, cautiously peered out one of the cabin windows to see what the commotion was all about. The moon was just beginning to rise, and she could make out several shadows darting back and forth outside the cabin. She also heard several of the boys laughing, so she suspected that it was some of the other campers playing a prank on them. She decided to yell out a warning.

"All right, you guys! If you don't stop this stupidness right now, I'm going to tell Pastor Randy!"

The boys froze in their tracks when they heard Cally's commanding voice.

Stanley called to the boys that it was time for them to get out of there and to get back to their cabin.

The nearly full moon was now just above the distant treetops. And when Stanley and the other boys turned to run back to their cabin, they received the shock of a lifetime. A huge creature possibly eight feet tall was clearly silhouetted in the moonlight. Its eyes glowed red from the reflected light, and it was advancing toward them, preventing them from going directly to the cabin.

Stanley screamed, "Bigfoot! Let's get out of here!" He made a mad dash for the shoreline of Moose Lake, hoping to make a circuitous route around the creature and back to the safety of the cabin. The other boys hurried behind him.

Some of the boys smacked into trees in their hurry to escape, but eventually they all made it to Moose Lake.

Along the shoreline, the group of boys was trying to huddle together in a mass for protection while also trying to run to their cabin as fast as they could. The problem though was that they kept stepping on the heels of the sneakers of the person in front of them, causing the sneakers to come off. As the boys reached down for their sneakers, they tripped up the fellows behind them.

Soon the group was sprawled on the shoreline, desperately trying to shove their sneakers back upon their feet so they could get running again.

A growl from the woods caused them to look up in terror. The creature was still coming toward them. Its eyes gleamed eerily in the moonlight.

The boys screamed then ran in single-file toward their cabin. Some of them still carried their sneakers.

Stanley, panting and puffing, was the last one to leave the lake but not by choice. As he was about to turn and flee, a motion out on the lake caught his attention. In the brilliant moonlight reflected upon the rippling waters of Moose Lake, the ghostly figure of a girl floated toward him. Stanley was so scared he couldn't move.

Except for one thing—a growl nearby brought him back to reality. Stanley, with bulging eyes, glanced from the ghostly figure to the giant creature and back again. Then he ran as fast as he could to his cabin. Now he was very glad that he had brought plenty of clean underwear to camp!

Chapter 3

The boys in cabin number six spent a sleepless night in their bunk beds. Most of them had had the covers pulled over their heads, expecting at any moment for the giant creature—probably a Bigfoot—to come crashing through the cabin door.

Now it was time to begin another day, and the boys willingly got out of bed glad that the night was over and hoping that the creature was gone.

Surprisingly none of the boys was tired from not having slept. They cautiously peered out of the cabin windows into the gray dawn of the early morning to see if anything out there was moving.

Nothing was.

So, they showered and dressed and left the cabin to meet up with the other campers at morning devotions.

Stanley let the other boys go on ahead of him. Then he anxiously retraced his steps to the shore of Moose Lake. He wondered if the things he'd seen last night were actually an illusion. The big creature though had also been seen by the other boys, so he doubted if that had been an illusion. But the ghostly girl floating over the water— well, he had apparently been the only one to see that apparition—and maybe it had only been his imagination.

His thoughts were interrupted as he glanced down at the water's edge and distinctively saw a number of large tracks in the mud. Stanley couldn't tell bear tracks from other animal tracks. He just knew that these ones were big. There must have been some kind of creature down at the water's edge last night. But just what it was, he didn't know.

Stanley left the shoreline and hurried a bit to get to morning devotions on time. He arrived at the same time that Pastor Randy did.

"Morning, Stanley!" Pastor Randy spoke as they met.

Stanley slightly nodded his acknowledgement of the youth pastor then went into the building and sat down with some of the other boys from his cabin.

Roger was seated just behind him. He now leaned forward and asked Stanley what all the commotion had been about last night.

"What commotion?" Stanley whispered, almost hissing the words.

"Ah, c'mon, man!" Roger whispered back. "There was so much yelling and running around last night in the direction of cabins six and seven that it must have involved you!"

Stanley knew that the boys' excursion from cabin six was now known. To what extent it was known was now the big question. Roger's cabin was number five. Did others know too? From Pastor Randy's seemingly innocent greeting of him this morning, Stanley guessed that at least he didn't know about what had happened last night.

Stanley decided to play it lowkey with Roger. "Yeah, man! Me and the boys from cabin six raided the girls' cabin seven last night. It was a blast! You should have seen it too. We had them screamin,' thinkin' a Bigfoot was attacking their cabin."

Roger grinned a big grin. "Man, I knew it! I wish I had been there. Next time, get me too. Okay?"

Stanley nodded his assent.

Pastor Randy started the devotion time with some choruses. He then gave a short talk and ended with a prayer. He was about to dismiss the group to breakfast when the skinny boy Clarence spoke up in his "squeaky" voice. "Uh, Pastor Randy?"

"Yes, Clarence. What would you like to tell me?"

"Well last night we saw something strange out in the woods!"

"You mean you saw something out in the woods from your cabin, or you were out in the woods when you saw this strange thing?"

Clarence caught the drift of Pastor Randy's question and knew he was in a bind. Furthermore, he glanced around at the boys from cabin six and saw the scowls on their faces. Pastor Randy noticed the same thing.

Now most of the boys from cabin six had agreed not to tell anybody about what they had seen last night, especially since they could all get in trouble for raiding the girls' cabin number seven. But since the guys thought that Clarence was a geek, they generally stayed away from him, and therefore neglected to let him in on their decision not to tell anyone.

Clarence realized his mistake too late. He tried to wriggle out of the situation by downplaying what he had actually seen. "Well, I think we maybe saw a bear when we came back from campfire service last evening," he lied.

Cally rolled her eyes. But she and the other girls from cabin seven had decided not to snitch on the boys just yet. Anyway, it looked like they might be in big enough trouble at the moment.

Pastor Randy knew that more had gone on last night than what Clarence was telling him, but he let the situation go for now. He would try to find out more later. "Well, you all be careful. As I said yesterday morning, there may be a bear in the area." He then dismissed everyone to breakfast.

* * * * *

Sitting around the breakfast table, the boys from cabin six made it plain to Clarence that he was not to squeal on them. They then ate a hurried breakfast and left Clarence sitting by himself.

Buddy noticed him all alone and realized he still had time before his first class, so he decided to join him at the table. "Hi, Clarence. Mind if I sit with you?"

"Oh, hi, Buddy. Sure, I don't mind."

Buddy sat down on the bench next to Clarence. "I kind of noticed that the guys from your cabin were scowling at you," he said with concern. "Is everything all right?"

Clarence didn't reply right away. But then he looked Buddy in the eye and said, "You won't tell the guys from my cabin if I share something with you, will you, Buddy?"

"No, of course not!" Buddy assured him. "You can tell me anything."

"Well last night us guys were out raiding the girls' cabin number seven when suddenly we saw a large, I mean really large, creature with red eyes. It was coming at us, and it was growling! I think it might have been a Bigfoot!"

"A Bigfoot?" Buddy asked in surprise.

"Look, man, it wasn't a bear. Or at least it didn't look like any bear that I've seen in pictures. The only other large creature that walks on its hind legs that I've heard about is a Bigfoot. What else could it have been?"

"I don't know," Buddy said thoughtfully. "I never thought that a Bigfoot was real."

"I didn't either," Clarence replied. "Until last night! And I mean it was coming right for us!"

Buddy glanced at his wristwatch. "It's about time for us to get to our first class, Clarence. But hey, man, I'll try to see what I can find out, okay?"

Clarence nodded.

The two parted company, leaving in different directions since their respective classes were in buildings opposite from one another. Buddy was heading toward his class when he noticed Pastor Randy walking in a line that would intercept his own course of travel in just a few seconds. He called out to the youth pastor.

"Hi, Pastor Randy!"

The youth pastor came to a stop at the point where their paths met. "Why, hello, Buddy! Say, I noticed you sitting next to Clarence a few minutes ago. Is he all right?"

Buddy hesitated a few seconds before responding. Actually, he had promised Clarence that he would not rat on him to the boys in cabin six. He hadn't promised to not tell Pastor Randy. He decided now that he should tell the youth pastor about what Clarence had said. "I'm not real sure if he is all right," Buddy replied. "He seemed worried about what the boys in cabin six might do to him if he revealed any of their secret whereabouts last night."

"Ah, so that's it," Pastor Randy said, nodding his head. "The guys were out of their cabin last night. Probably they were trying to pull some kind of a prank."

"But Clarence seemed even more upset about what he claims the guys saw when they were outside their cabin," Buddy said, kicking the toe of his sneaker in the dirt.

"What did he claim they saw?" Pastor Randy inquired, wrinkling up his brow.

"He claims the boys saw a large upright creature with red eyes that was growling and coming to get them," Buddy said, squinting his eyes at the youth pastor. "He said also that he thought it might be a Bigfoot."

"He said what?" Pastor Randy's face now was serious.

"Clarence said he thought they saw a Bigfoot," Buddy reaffirmed.

Pastor Randy rubbed his chin for several moments. "Do you remember, Buddy, that I said I saw tracks down by the lake shore at devotions yesterday morning?"

"Yeah," Buddy replied slowly.

"Well, what I didn't say is that those tracks looked more like huge human footprints than a bear's prints."

The hair on the back of Buddy's neck stood up. "You don't really believe a Bigfoot lives in this area, do you?" he asked with alarm.

Pastor Randy shrugged his shoulders. "You'd better get to class," he suggested to Buddy.

After Buddy was gone, Pastor Randy decided to go back to Moose Lake and study the shoreline again. When he got to the place on the lake opposite his cabin, he carefully observed the tracks he had seen yesterday morning. He then walked along the shoreline for a couple of hundred yards more until he was nearly opposite cabin six. There he spotted another set of similar-looking tracks. Something surely made these tracks. But what? He decided to follow the tracks back into the woods. He was able to make them out plainly while they were in soft dirt. But soon the tracks were less discernable as the ground became harder and was covered with leaves. After a short while, Pastor Randy couldn't find any more of the tracks, so he decided to go back to camp. On the way back, he thought about calling in some experts to analyze the tracks. Maybe that would give them some answers.

* * * * *

Linda Chambers was on Highway 27, traveling to Northridge, the nearest city with a good-sized grocery store. This was where she usually did her grocery shopping, and she enjoyed the pleasant forty-minute drive through the beautiful countryside. Today, besides getting the usual groceries for the upcoming week, she was planning on getting a few extra items as a special treat for Buddy and Cally when they returned home from camp.

She had received her first letter from the kids just this morning and that had reminded her to get the cake mix and ice cream for them as a homecoming welcome. The letter had said that they both were fine. One thing, however, had disturbed her more than she was willing to admit. A boy named Stanley was trying to be a bully to Buddy and Cally and some of the other campers. "Trying to be a bully" was the way Buddy had written it in his letter. Apparently, Stanley hadn't really succeeded in his attempts at being a bully, but that didn't mean he wouldn't succeed by the time camp was over. Buddy had written to her not to worry. But of course, being a mom, she couldn't help it.

Mrs. Chambers's thoughts were disrupted as she noticed the sign that pointed to Camp Musky. She turned her head to peer down the same gravel road that she and her family had traveled on several days ago when Buddy and Cally had been taken to the camp. Already she missed them.

The SUV was now halfway to Northridge. In another ten miles, she would pass through the town of Moose Lake, and then another ten miles after that would bring her to Wilson's IGA in Northridge.

The last twenty minutes of the drive to her destination were filled with wonderful thoughts as she remembered her own happy times spent at Camp Musky when she was a teen. Indeed, that is where she had met Dave, her husband now of fifteen years.

A smile was still faintly etched onto Mrs. Chambers's face when she clicked on her right blinker and turned the SUV into the IGA parking lot. She shut off the motor and then fumbled around in her purse for her shopping list. Retrieving it, she got out and locked the vehicle. Then she went into the store.

She found a shopping cart and began pushing it. Of course, it had to have a squeaky wheel.

The first item on her list was milk. She put a gallon of two percent into the cart. Next was bread—then lunch meat, mayo, cheese. Mrs. Chambers was rounding the next aisle for cake mix when she noticed a tall, thin man in a black suit, standing in the middle of the aisle with his back to her. He was talking to an elderly gentleman whom she recognized as Mr. Capner, the editor of the *Northridge Daily Journal, the city's newspaper.*

"I hear that strange footprints have been seen at Camp Musky," the tall man in the black suit was telling Mr. Capner.

Even though Mrs. Chambers hadn't seen Horace Chillblaines in several years, she instantly recognized his shrill voice. She quickly backed her cart up and went down the next aisle, coming to a stop where she judged the two men were standing in the adjacent aisle. She listened intently.

"What kind of footprints do they think they are?" Mr. Capner asked.

"Well, some believe that a Bigfoot might be living in the area. The tracks are huge, but they look more human than anything else."

"A Bigfoot!" Mr. Capner was incredulous. "Surely, you're joking!"

"All I know is what I've heard," Horace replied, speaking more shrilly than before.

"Wait a minute, Horace," Mr. Capner commanded as he reached into his jacket pocket for a pad and pen. "This might make a good story for tomorrow's edition. Okay, tell me again what you said you heard out at Camp Musky."

Horace Chillblaines did so with apparent pleasure.

Mrs. Chambers hurriedly finished her shopping and went through the checkout line. After depositing her groceries onto the back seat of the SUV, she sat in the front seat trying to make sense out of what she had just heard.

"Bigfoot tracks seen out at Camp Musky?" she mused to herself. "That can't be true." But what if it was?

She decided to go to the camp on her way back and find out first hand. If a Bigfoot really did exist, and it lived around the campsite, then everybody there could be in danger. She thought of Buddy and Cally being torn apart by a wild, giant animal, and she pressed too hard on the accelerator as she started to leave. The SUV burned a black streak onto the IGA parking lot. Then she turned left onto Highway 27, cutting in front of a pickup with "Bigfoot" tires. The driver laid on his horn.

"Oh, brother," Mrs. Chambers thought as she glanced at the tires, then left Northridge in a rush, accelerating through a yellow light, and going well beyond the speed limit of sixty miles per hour as she sped out onto the open highway.

She would have made it to Moose Lake in eight minutes instead of the usual ten except that she never made it there at all. Rounding a bend in the highway and with her tires squealing, she glimpsed a large, black creature coming out of the trees and heading for the highway in front of her. She hit her brakes hard, and the last thing she remembered was the creature's huge, black hairy form as she collided with it and then rolled the SUV over an embankment.

*****

The Sheriff's CB radio was "squawking," as orders from a dispatcher were being sent to him. Red and blue lights flashed from the top of his patrol car which was parked on the shoulder of Highway 27 where Mrs. Chambers's vehicle had gone over the side of the road.

The person who had called in the accident had happened to be a doctor returning to Northridge. He and the Deputy Sheriff Don Phillips from the same city were assisting Mrs. Chambers, who was unconscious but at least alive.

Off in the distance, the siren of an ambulance was heard screaming the announcement of its soon-to-be arrival.

Deputy Sheriff Phillips cut the safety belt off of Mrs. Chambers with his pocket knife, since the locking mechanism of the belt had become jammed. Dr. Thomson then felt her vital signs and checked for broken bones before he and the deputy sheriff carefully removed her from the SUV, carried her up the embankment, and laid her on a blanket on the grassy bank off from the highway.

Meanwhile, Sheriff Greene was examining the tire marks on the road's pavement where the vehicle had rolled off the highway. He noticed some blood and black hair on the road where the vehicle had begun its departure from the highway and had headed toward the embankment. He thought that maybe Mrs. Chambers had hit a skunk or some other small animal on the road, causing the accident. But no creature's body was anywhere in the vicinity.

Soon the ambulance skidded to a stop behind the sheriff's patrol car. The EMTs brought out a stretcher, carefully placed Mrs. Chambers on it, and put her into the vehicle. Then the trio of cars made its way back to Northridge with the patrol car in the lead and Dr. Thomson's car in the rear.

*****

It was swim time at Camp Musky. Buddy had gotten special permission to go fishing today instead of just the usual swimming. Since he would be away from the other swimmers and still would be in sight of the lifeguard, the permission had been granted. So he took a rowboat out onto the lake. Cally had never been fishing before, so she decided to go along with her brother.

They took along two of the camp's fishing rods and a tackle box of assorted lures, plugs, jigs, spinners, and spoons. Cally sat in the front of the boat while Buddy rowed it out away from shore. Soon after Buddy had showed his sister how to cast her rod, they were flipping lures toward the shoreline in hopes of catching some bass or other predatory fish.

Cast, plunk, retrieve. Cast, plunk, retrieve. Both anglers were getting into a sort of rhythm when suddenly the line grew taut on Buddy's rod. A feisty, five-pound bass exploded on the surface of the lake and did a "tail dance" upon the water before diving back into the green pool below. The line on Buddy's rod "zinged" as it sped off the reel after the big fish. The tip of Buddy's rod was bent nearly double when it abruptly straightened out, the line going limp.

"Rats!" he exclaimed with bitter disappointment. "I just lost him!"

"That's too bad, Bud!" Cally tried to soothe her brother's feelings. Just then, however, she received a hard strike from a nice fish, and the battle was on.

Meanwhile, Buddy reeled up his line thinking some weeds were caught on his lure since there was a slight drag on the rod. But when he lifted the lure out of the water, about half of the bass' head was still on it.

"What in the world?" he thought to himself, not realizing that a larger predatory fish had chomped the bass off at its head. He stared at the partial bass head dangling from his line.

Cally had almost played her fish to the side of the boat when suddenly her line went slack as well. Disappointed, she lifted the line out of the water but nothing was on it.

Buddy had just tossed the remnant piece of fish head into the lake when Cally turned to him and said, "Hey, bro, I think I've fished enough for now. I'm going to go in for a little swim."

Both of them had their swimsuits on, and this had been their original plan: to fish awhile, and then go swimming. Buddy was still musing over the strange situation with the fish since in all his years of fishing he had never experienced an incident such as this before. He barely heard what Cally had said to him. But when her words finally dawned on his mind, she was already diving over the side of the boat. At that instant, another thought struck him full force.

"Cal, don't go into the water!" he urgently commanded. But it was too late.

Splash! A few seconds later, Cally surfaced from her dive. "What did you yell out at me, Bud?" she asked, squinting at him as the overhead sun was almost directly in her eyes.

"I yelled for you not to go into the water!" Buddy replied. His words still had an urgency to them.

"Why?" Cally inquired, beginning to feel a little anxious at her brother's tone of voice.

"Because, something weird is—" He stopped in midsentence and directed his gaze a short distance from his sister. "Don't move, Cal!" he slowly whispered. His eyes riveted on something behind her.

Cally was now scared out of her wits. She didn't dare ask what the danger was, and she didn't dare turn around to see what it was. But she couldn't be perfectly still either. To stay afloat, she must tread water, which she did as gingerly as she could.

A giant musky—the musky—was several yards away from Cally. It was fully six feet long, floating just under the surface of the lake, and its tail section was bent in a semicircle as muskies will sometimes do when examining a possible prey.

Buddy was at a loss to know what to do. He didn't know for instance if whacking the fish with an oar would scare it away or cause it to strike Cally. On the other hand, if he did nothing, it might strike anyway.

"Cal," he spoke as calmly as he could. "Slowly come to the boat."

Actually, by treading water, Cally had been automatically advancing toward the rowboat. In a few more seconds, she was able to reach the edge of one side of the boat with her left hand.

The musky had remained motionless all this while.

Buddy extended his right hand and caught hold of his sister's right one as well. With this help, Cally was able to raise her body up and slide her legs over the boat's side and then roll into the craft.

The boat rocked hard but finally righted itself.

Cally felt paralyzed from the exertion and fright of the experience. And for a moment, she couldn't move. But then, curiosity got the best of her, and she lifted her head to see over the side of the boat as she asked her brother, "What did you see in the water that almost got me, Bud?"

"I think it was the monster musky that Stanley and his dad had told us about. Man, Cally, it was huge!"

Both siblings scanned the surface of the lake to try to get a glimpse of the big fish, but it was gone. A couple of times they thought they felt a "bump" on the underside of the boat as if the musky was still playing with them, but it might have been just their imaginations or the waves from the lake.

"Let's get back to land," Buddy finally said.

This time Cally picked up the oars and rowed, especially since she had a lot of adrenaline to use up.

In a short time, they were back at the shore. They were headed for the cafeteria to see if they could find Pastor Randy and tell him about the incident when Dr. Ravenbush intercepted them. "Buddy. Cally. There's an urgent phone call for you guys in the registration room. It's from your dad."

"What's it about?" the siblings asked at the same time.

"He didn't say, but it really sounded urgent!"

The pair, having forgotten all about the episode with the musky, hurried over to the registration room. Buddy grabbed the phone which was dangling by its cord from a wall mount.

"Hello, Dad? What's up?" Buddy's face was blank as he listened for several moments to his dad's voice on the other end of the line. "Oh, no!" he groaned.

Cally came closer, bending her head down, trying to hear her dad's comments through the receiver.

"Okay, Dad, we'll be ready when you get here!" Buddy hung up the phone. His face was white, and he was blinking back some tears.

"What is it, Buddy?" Cally asked anxiously as she rubbed her hands together.

Buddy looked down at the floor and then slowly lifted his eyes to stare directly into Cally's. "Mom's been in an accident. The SUV went off the road, and she's now in the hospital center in Northridge. Dad will be here in a little bit to pick us up."

Cally bit her lower lip which had started to quiver. Tears streamed down her ashen cheeks, and she crumpled down into one of the cushioned chairs in the room. Buddy sat in another chair opposite her. So much had happened in such a short while that his mind began to reel. Pictures of Bigfoot, a giant musky, the Chillblaines mansion, and the SUV going off the road became blended in a terrifying scene which seemed like a nightmare. Only now he couldn't wake up from it all. With difficulty, he forced the scenes from his mind.

"Cal," Buddy spoke to his still-sobbing sister. "Maybe we should pray."

She nodded without saying a word.

Together they held hands while Buddy spoke a heartfelt prayer, asking the Lord to please help their mom and to also comfort them, especially Cally. After that, they both felt some better.

Mr. Chambers had called on his cell phone when he was only about ten minutes away from Camp Musky. So now just a short time later, he pulled up in front of the registration cabin in his pickup truck, having come directly from his work.

The siblings hurried out to meet with him at his rolled-down cab window.

"Hi, guys," Mr. Chambers said, trying to sound optimistic. "Hop in the truck. I'll take you to your cabins where you can get changed. Then we'll see Mom at the hospital."

They climbed into the truck cab, and Mr. Chambers took them to their cabins. About ten minutes later after changing and getting back into the pickup, Buddy and Cally were riding down the long gravel driveway of Camp Musky toward the Northridge Hospital.

Except for a few initial comments by Dad to break the tension, the trio rode in silence. After turning onto Highway 27, the tires on the pickup "hummed" on the pavement, creating a background noise that droned into their subconscious minds.

Each of the three family members was deep into his or her own thoughts. Even the scenery going by seemed surreal.

About 5:15 p.m., they entered Northridge. Mr. Chambers slowed down the pickup to the now lawful speed limit of thirty-five miles per hour. The hospital was on the other side of town, so the impatient trio could do nothing else except to wait out the torturous minutes it took to get there.

And prayed!

CHAPTER 4

Soon the hospital came into view. A few seconds later, Mr. Chambers pulled the pickup into one of the parking slots that said "Visitor" on the pavement. Buddy and Cally were exiting the passenger side door before Dad had turned the engine off. But they waited for him in the parking lot before going into the hospital.

Just ahead of them, the Chambers could see a gurney being pushed through the emergency entrance doors by paramedics. Mom must have been taken into the hospital on just such a gurney, they thought to themselves.

By now, the Chambers had reached the main entrance door to the hospital. They entered silently and in single file. Dad held the door open for the youngsters to go through. Dad then led the way to the information desk.

"May I help you?" the receptionist at the desk asked, looking up with a smile.

"Uh, yes, please," Dad replied a little hesitantly, glancing at Buddy and Cally. "We would like to see Linda Chambers if we may."

"Are you relatives of hers?" the receptionist asked, still smiling.

"Yes, I'm her husband, and these two are our children."

"Let's see... Linda Chambers is on the ICU floor, room number two. And yes, you may see her," the receptionist said a little robotically. Or so it seemed to Buddy. At least, she was nice if not overly concerned, he thought.

"The ICU is on floor number three," the receptionist called after them as they headed to the elevators.

Dad pushed the green arrow button on elevator number one, and they all watched the lighted numbers above the elevator door go from four down to one. There was a loud "ding," and the elevator door opened. A middle-aged man and a woman who apparently was his wife were wiping the tears from their eyes as they stepped off the elevator and brushed past the Chambers.

Cally muffled a cry by putting a hand to her mouth as they all stared at the man and the woman as they left the hospital.

The Chambers entered elevator number one, and Dad pushed button number three on the wall. As the doors slid closed, he hugged his children and assured them that everything would be all right.

The elevator came to a stop at floor number three. They exited the doors and turned right, following an arrow that told them where room two was located. As they came to the room, they noticed that the curtains were drawn, and they heard activity going on inside.

A couple of minutes went by, and then a nurse pulled the curtains back and came out of the room. She smiled at the Chambers. "Are you relatives of Linda Chambers," she asked when she saw the concern on their faces.

"Yes, I'm her husband, and these are our two children," Dad explained for the second time this evening.

"Well, I was just applying some bandages," the nurse explained. "You can see her, but she isn't conscious right now," she added cautiously, looking at Buddy and Cally.

The three entered Mrs. Chambers's room and were shocked to see Mom lying on the hospital bed, her face swollen and purple from the bruises that she had received. A tube had been inserted into her mouth, as well as oxygen hoses into her nostrils. Her vital signs were portrayed upon a monitor, and the steady *blip, blip, blip,* on the screen indicated that at least her heartbeat was still strong.

Mr. Chambers, Buddy, and Cally stood around Mom's bed for quite some time, holding hands and not speaking. Finally, Dad suggested that they all sit down in the chairs that had been provided for the visitors who came into this room. They prayed together and prayed individually, got up from their chairs to stand by Mom's bedside, and then sat down in them again. Sometimes they dozed off while sitting in the chairs. This went on through most of the night.

Dawn was beginning to pale in the east, and Dad told the kids he should take them back to camp, and also that he should go to work. They would see Mom again soon. As they turned to leave, Mrs. Chambers stirred a bit. In another couple of minutes, her eyes opened, and the three other family members rushed back to her bedside. They gently hugged her and told her how much they loved her.

It was obvious that Linda Chambers could not speak right now. She weakly motioned her hand to a pad of paper and a pen that was located on her tray. Dad brought them to her. He clicked the pen and held the pad for her as she slowly wrote some words. The first words read, "I love you all too." Then she wrote in as few words as possible about what she had heard from Horace Chillblaines in the store concerning a possible Bigfoot sighting at Camp Musky. Having worn herself out with the writing, Mrs. Chambers dropped the pen.

"Okay, honey," Dave told his wife, "You better rest now. We'll check out the story of the Bigfoot sighting. I need to get the kids back to camp, and I need to go to work. We'll be back to see you as soon as we can. He gave her a kiss as did Buddy and Cally.

After a brief breakfast in the hospital cafeteria, Mr. Chambers dropped the siblings off at their respective cabins at Camp Musky and then left them to go to his job.

Though the Chambers kids were pretty tired, they had decided to go to devotions this morning. After first taking quick showers and getting changed, they met together on the trail leading to the camp's cafeteria. A few of the other campers were also heading in that direction. Buddy and Cally explained to them about their mom's situation to which they expressed their heartfelt condolences.

They had almost made it to the cafeteria when suddenly Stanley and his friend Roger came hurrying up from behind them and pushed their way through the entrance door almost knocking Cally over.

"Hey, man, watch it!" Buddy sternly spoke as he grabbed Cally by the arm.

Stanley turned, and with a sneer, he said, "I heard about your mom being in an accident, Chambers. And you know what? I hope she dies just like my mom did!"

Buddy and Cally stood horrified as they watched Stanley and Roger walk through the cafeteria door. Then they took their seats as far away from that rude duo as they could.

Just then, Pastor Randy entered the cafeteria and looked with great concern at the Chambers kids. He said, "We all need to pray for Buddy and Cally's mom, Mrs. Chambers, who as everyone knows is in the Northridge Hospital. I know that you guys made her a visit last night. How is she doing?"

Buddy hesitated a moment, still stinging inside from Stanley's cruel remark, then he said, "She came out of her coma this morning, but she still looks pretty bad. I hope she's going to be all right, but we're not completely sure yet." He glanced over at Cally.

Pastor Randy then led the campers in a time of prayer for Mrs. Chambers with each one who felt like it joining in one by one.

After they had finished praying, Pastor Randy picked up the morning newspaper he had brought with him and showed everyone the front-page headlines. It read, "Bigfoot Tracks Spotted at Camp Musky!"

"Now I wonder where the newspaper got its so-called information from?" Pastor Randy inquired as he looked around the room, especially at Stanley and the boys from cabin six. "Does anyone know?" he added.

Almost all the campers shrugged their shoulders or shook their heads to show that they didn't know how that "information" got into this morning's edition of the *Daily Journal*.

Pastor Randy continued, "The article says that an anonymous source was responsible for the facts relating to the story. Can anyone tell me who that anonymous source is?"

Buddy raised his hand to get the youth pastor's attention. "Uh, Pastor Randy. When we were at the hospital my mom came out of her coma like I had mentioned earlier. She wasn't able to speak, but she was able to write something for us. She wrote that she remembered going shopping yesterday. And while she was in the store, she overheard Horace Chillblaines telling Mr. Capner, the editor of the *Daily Journal*, that he had heard that Bigfoot tracks had been seen at Camp Musky."

"Horace Chillblaines?" Pastor Randy's lower jaw fell open, and his eyebrows looked like they were going to break from arching too much. "So that's how all this got into the *Daily Journal*. First, the Chillblaines want to shut down Camp Musky, then Horace tells Mr. Capner that he heard Bigfoot tracks were seen here. What are the Chillblaines trying to do?"

Buddy didn't know what the Chillblaines were really up to, but he did intend to find out and soon too.

The group then sang a few choruses, and Pastor Randy gave a short devotional talk, and then dismissed everyone to breakfast.

*****

George Nutter and Fred Pringle were the two biology teachers at Northridge Community College. They were the nearest to being wildlife "experts" with which Pastor Randy could get. He had called them earlier to travel out to Camp Musky and investigate the big tracks by Moose Lake, and to see if they could determine what made them. George and Fred now seemed to be greatly bewildered by what they saw, and they expressed that bewilderment to each other in their conversation.

"Hey, Fred, have you ever seen tracks like these before?" George asked the question and then whistled his amazement before his companion answered.

"Man, I've never seen tracks so long and wide even from a bear," Fred replied, staring at the giant impressions in the mud. "What do you think made them?"

"I dunno," George said, taking his cap off his head and brushing his matted hair back with his fingers. "I mean, I've heard stories all my life about folks seeing big ape-like creatures in these woods. But I guess I've always just assumed that they were tall tales."

"Well anyway, we should make some plaster casts of the tracks," Fred advised. "Then we can take our time studying them back at the college."

"Yeah, that's a good idea," George responded.

They both went back to the truck and got the materials ready to make the casts. First, they mixed some water in with the plaster powder to get a gooey mix that they could pour into several of the tracks. Then after making the casts, they waited until the plaster was dried and hardened. Finally, they lifted the casts out of the tracks and wrapped them in plastic bubble wrap to keep them from getting broken and then placed them into a cardboard box in the back of the truck.

"Well, that takes care of that!" Fred spoke with satisfaction at their having completed the task.

George nodded and then said, "What do you think we should do now, Fred?"

Fred stared at the ground for several seconds before he answered. "M-maybe we should follow the tracks to see where they lead to. What do you think, George?"

"I don't know if that's such a good idea.

We didn't bring our rifles with us, and what if we stumble on to the creature?" George's voice was a few notes higher than usual, indicating his nervousness.

"Yeah. But think of the thrill we'd get if we caught a glimpse of this big boy running through the woods," Fred said rather dreamily. "All we'd need to do is carry a couple of good-sized sticks with us. And if the animal started to charge us, we could beat the trees and brush with the sticks and scare it away."

"I don't know," George hesitated.

"Aw, c'mon," Fred insisted. "What an opportunity for science! I've got my camera in the truck. And if we could get a snapshot of a Bigfoot, we'd put Camp Musky on the map!"

George reluctantly gave in to Fred's suggestion. They each cut a hefty stick with Fred's hatchet that he kept in the back of the truck. Then taking along the camera, they slowly followed the tracks into the woods until they couldn't see any more of them.

At that point, they decided to split up with the hope of covering more territory, and thus, increase their chances of seeing the creature. Each went the opposite way around a small hill.

George, who was more than a little out of shape, was panting and perspiring when he got to the top of a second hill so that he could see out farther. Fred was nowhere to be seen. George continued his way into the forest. Cautiously and with some anxiety, he tiptoed slowly forward so as to try to not make a sound. About a half hour later, he suddenly realized that he had no idea where he was. Panic began to set in, and he took off running through the brush, trying to find Fred.

Meanwhile Fred, who had been intent on his search for the creature, abruptly began hearing something thrashing through the woods. It sounded quite large too. He readied his camera for a quick shot.

Click! The camera flashed into George's face as he came through a clump of trees.

Whack! George's stick clubbed Fred on the head as he rushed out of the clump of trees.

Fred fell heavily to the ground and lay there unconscious.

George, still startled by the flash and scared out of his mind, clubbed Fred a couple of times on the ribs before he realized what he was doing. "Fred! Fred! Are you all, right?" he asked absentmindedly not knowing what else to say. He knelt down by Fred and reality dawned upon him at that instant. Frightened by what he had just done to his friend, he gently propped Fred's head against a tree. "Fred, can you hear me?"

Fred groaned a little, and he started to stir. "Oh! I'm hurt all over," he muttered, opening his eyes and holding his side. "What happened to me?"

"Well," George hesitated. "I-I thought you were a Bigfoot closing in on me, and I guess I hit you pretty hard with my stick."

"It feels like some of my ribs are broken," Fred wheezed.

"Can you walk?" George asked gingerly, pressing lightly on Fred's ribs with the tips of his fingers.

"Ouch! Don't touch my ribs, George! I told you. I think some of them are broken! And no, I don't think I can walk. I'm not sure I can even get to my feet. The pain is just too great when I move."

"Well, I'm not sure which way to go anyway, Fred, even if you could move. I'm kind of lost out here."

"I certainly don't know where we are," Fred replied disgustedly. "I was knocked unconscious, and when I came to, I lost all concept of direction!" He rolled his eyes and turned his face away.

"I guess we'll just have to stay right here until help comes for us," George said decidedly. "You can't move, and I'm not going off without you!" he added with a nervous glance around.

"I guess," Fred said.

*****

Lunch was just over, and the afternoon activity for the day was a hike in the woods. This was usually the big outdoor event at Camp Musky for each year. The campers, all of whom were going on the hike, were expected to collect samples of the mineral and plant life in the area, and sometimes they were "treated" to a sighting of deer or other animals on the hike.

Even Stanley Foster enjoyed going on this afternoon walk. It gave him a chance to think up new pranks to play on some of the other campers. He and his buddy Roger were looking for walking sticks to assist them on the hike just now. After finding a couple, they started in jousting, pretending they were medieval knights. Stanley got a pretty good jab in the stomach which knocked him to the ground. This made him mad. And after getting up, he began twirling and swinging his stick at Roger like he was a ninja warrior. Roger parried the blows with his own stick, but a couple of the blows struck him on the knuckles, and he started getting mad as well. An all-out fight would have occurred except that Pastor Randy saw them and put a stop to it.

Soon the two boys were friends again, and they joined the group of campers going on the hike. But they decided they'd be last so that they could have a good look at everybody in front of them and possibly be able to do a little mischief.

Buddy and Cally were about in the center of the group, and a counsellor named Janet was leading the hikers. She started them off at a leisurely pace so that everyone could get accustomed to the walking uphill, downhill, and through the brush that extended, at times, onto the hiking trail. She didn't want the hikers getting tired too soon, or they might get discouraged and go back to camp. At times, they stopped not only for periods of rest, but so that the hikers could collect the nature samples and put them in their backpacks.

Stanley and Roger rolled a large rock over to see what was under it. A small garter snake began slithering away, but the two delighted boys caught it before it could do so. Holding it behind his back,

Stanley strolled over to where Cally was intently looking for her own specimens to collect. He brought his hand forward and said to her, "Hey, look, Cally! I've brought you a present!"

She glanced up just in time to see the writhing snake that Stanley was holding. The next instant, Stanley let go of the snake, and it dropped squirming on top of her head. Ordinarily, Cally wasn't the least bit afraid of a little garter snake. But having it dropped on her head so abruptly startled her to say the least. She shrieked then caught hold of the snake by the tail and flung it as far away from her as she could.

The snake sailed through the air and then flopped onto their leader Janet's neck and slid down the collar of her shirt and down her back. Janet shrieked, and she did what looked like an Indian war dance. She bobbed up and down, grabbing her shirttail and shaking it until the reptile fell to the ground and slithered away as fast as it could go.

"Who threw that snake at me?" Janet demanded, looking toward the area from where the "flying" snake had come. She noticed Cally staring at her blankly as if in disbelief. Then she glanced behind the girl to where Stanley and Roger were standing, each having a big smirk upon his face.

"All right," Janet was now glowering. "Which one of you three threw that snake at me?"

Stanley and Roger both pointed at Cally.

"Is that right, Cally? Did you throw that snake at me?" Janet asked with an obvious frown upon her face.

"Y-yes, ma'am," Cally replied meekly. "B-but you see, it was an accident."

"An accident?" Janet was now glaring at Cally with her hands upon her hips. "How on earth can you throw a snake at someone by accident?"

Cally was about to answer, but Janet cut her off short.

"I think you're making up an excuse for pulling a prank on me, Cally! Just for that, I want you to go back to camp!"

Cally tried to answer again, but Janet wouldn't let her.

"Now, young lady!" Janet ordered, pointing in the direction of camp. "Get back to camp immediately! I'll deal with you later!"

Cally looked like she was about to cry.

Buddy came over to Janet after having seen the big commotion. "I'll go with her back to camp if you don't mind. I was her hiking partner anyway."

"That's fine!" Janet replied. She then turned around and had the other hikers return to the trail. Buddy and Cally walked the other way toward camp.

Stanley and Roger held their hands over their mouths so that no one could see them giggling. Finally, Roger said, "We'd better be getting back to the hike, or Janet may suspect us for being in on the prank."

Stanley thought for a few seconds. "Uh, why don't you go and catch up with the hikers, Rog. I think I left my walking stick back at the rock where we found the snake. I'll be along shortly."

"Okay, man," Roger said. "I'll see ya in a few seconds." He got back to the trail and started trotting.

Actually, Stanley wanted to climb a little hill that they had hiked around a bit earlier so that he could watch Buddy and Cally on their way back to camp. Somehow, he felt this would give him a little more satisfaction at seeing Cally being punished for something she didn't mean to do. He waited until Roger was out of sight and then left the trail and climbed to the top of the hill. The excursion left him winded so he stopped for a few seconds to catch his breath. By the time he searched for the pair returning to camp, he only got a glimpse of them as they faded in and out through some tree foliage. So, he walked a bit farther to see if he could get a better view of them.

Again, he only caught a glimpse of them through the trees and brush. Once again, he moved farther on.

This went on for about ten minutes until Stanley couldn't see the Chambers kids at all. He decided to return to the hiking trail except for one thing—Stanley had no clue where the hiking trail was.

*****

When Buddy and Cally came back to the camp, they found it practically deserted. All of the campers, except for them of course, were on the hike. Apparently, Pastor Randy, Dr. Ravenbush, and some of the other camp leaders were taking advantage of the campers being gone and were now napping or doing some other quiet activity.

Soon an idea came to Buddy. "Hey, Sis," he said with a sparkle in his eyes. "How about if we pay a visit to the Chillblaines's mansion?"

"What are you talking about?" Cally responded with a tone of surprise in her voice.

"Well, nobody would miss us around here and maybe, just maybe, we could find out some things that are puzzling a lot of people."

Cally thought about that for a moment. Then her eyes brightened. "You know, Bud, since the first day I saw that spooky, old mansion, I thought it would be kind of neat to explore it. Okay, let's do it."

"We need to make sure that the Chillblaines aren't home though," Buddy added carefully.

Cally nodded. "I've noticed a big black car parked in front of the mansion several times when we went to the campfire services. But one time, I noticed that it was gone. It must belong to the Chillblaines. Maybe we could wait until the car is gone and then go into their house."

"Yeah, that's a good idea, Cal. I've seen that car too. Let's take a quick walk up the campfire trail and see if the car is parked there now."

"But remember, Bud, there's two of the Chillblaines. What if only one of them takes the car someplace, and the other one stays home?"

"Hmmm," Buddy thought that one over. "Well, that is a possibility. But if I was one of the Chillblaines brothers, stuck out in that old mansion all day, I'd want to get out every chance I got. More than likely, they'd leave together nine out of ten times. I'd say the odds are in our favor if we see their car gone."

The Chambers kids jogged up the campfire trail until they could see the Chillblaines's mansion. They hid partially behind a tree, so it wouldn't be as obvious that they were staring at the mansion, should the Chillblaines be home and see them.

"I don't see the car in the yard!" Buddy said with excitement. Then he added, "Let's be careful though and hide as much as possible behind trees and other things as we approach the mansion."

Going from tree to shrub to rock to embankment, the two reached the mansion in about fifteen minutes. They circled to the back side of the house using an old white paint-weary picket fence for cover. Buddy told Cally to stay behind while he cautiously crept onto the back porch and tried the door. It was unlocked as he had expected it to be since the Chillblaines had such a bad reputation, lived in such isolation, and the mansion was so "spooky-looking" that nobody in his right mind would probably have dared to enter the house.

Buddy motioned for his sister to come onto the porch which she did. Then the two nervously pushed the door open and entered into that dark, musty-smelling mansion.

Suddenly the floorboards squeaked, and the two jumped. They both exhaled a long deep breath. Then their hearts having calmed down a bit, they resumed their exploration. The mansion on the inside seemed larger than it looked on the outside. But part of that may have been due to the many mirrors that adorned the walls of the old structure. Apparently every wall had its own mirror, and even in the relative darkness of the building, enough light was transmitted to their glassy surfaces to not only show the Chambers kids the direction to go but also to make the rooms seem enormous.

Buddy and Cally noticed a number of trophies and plaques on shelves, and certificates on the walls. They examined several of these and discovered that the Chillblaines brothers had been professors in a prestigious university. Horace had been a professor of religion, and Hector had been a professor of Christian history. This surprised the two greatly. They examined more of the plaques and trophies and also discovered that the two brothers had been honored on many occasions for civic works and community services. It didn't make sense why the brothers seemed so bitter about life, and especially why they were now so opposed to a Christian camp that they themselves had started years ago. But maybe they would find an answer to this dilemma if they kept looking.

The pair tiptoed along a hallway, edging toward another room. Suddenly the sound of a car's motor was heard coming up the lane toward the mansion. Buddy and Cally rushed to the nearest window and parted its curtains just enough to peer outside. With a surge of fear, they recognized the black vehicle that they had seen parked here before. It now came to a stop in front of the mansion.

"Oh no, Bud!" Cally exclaimed. "What are we going to do now? If we run outside, the Chillblaines are sure to see or hear us. But we can't stay here!"

Buddy knew she was right. At this very moment, he could see the two brothers getting out of their car. Even if the Chambers kids exited the back door they had come in through, the Chillblaines would most likely hear them stomping across the wooden deck. Buddy glanced desperately around the room. Through another hallway, he noticed a door that was partially opened. "C'mon, Cal! Maybe we can shut ourselves into a room and then escape out of a window without the Chillblaines noticing us!"

He grabbed her hand and pulled her down the hallway to the open door. When they got to the door, they realized with shock that it didn't lead to another regular room, but that it was the entrance way to the basement.

"We'd better go down there and hope there's an exit," Buddy whispered to his sister. They could hear the doorknob to the front door turning as they descended the basement stairs.

Chapter 5

"I thought we left the door to the basement closed," Horace wheezed as the Chillblaines brothers entered the mansion.

"I guess I forgot to close it after I stashed the gorilla suit down there," Hector replied.

Though the voices sounded muffled, Buddy and Cally, who now were on the basement floor, heard the term "gorilla suit," and they glanced at each other. Then they heard the basement door close, and they were in total darkness.

"Cally," Buddy whispered to his sister. "I think I saw some curtains covering the basement windows before the door was closed. Maybe we can open the curtains and let in some light down here."

"Good idea," Cally whispered back.

The two felt their way to one of the basement walls, and then they reached above their heads until they found a pair of curtains covering one of the basement's small windows. They parted the curtains and light instantly poured into the room. Now they could see to part several more pairs of curtains, which they did.

They both scanned the large room they were in. A closed door at the far end of the wall opposite them looked like a possible way of escape if it was only unlocked. They tiptoed over to it and to their great relief found that it was indeed unlocked.

"Just like the rest of the doors in this place," Buddy muttered. Then he turned to Cally. "I don't think we should make our escape just yet, Cal."

She stared at him in disbelief. "What do you mean? Are you loony, Bud? What if the Chillblaines come down here and find us?" She spoke a little louder than she meant to.

"Shhh!" Buddy whispered with his finger to his lips. "Well, Sis, the Chillblaines don't know we're down here, and the chances are that they won't come down right away since they closed the basement door only a few minutes ago. I mean, if they had intended to look for something, they probably would've done it when they first came home." Buddy wasn't convinced that what he'd just said made any sense, especially since Cally was still looking at him as if he'd gone crazy. "Anyway," he continued, "I'd like to explore down here for a bit and see if we can find that gorilla suit that was mentioned."

Cally wanted to exit the basement door and get out of there as quickly as possible, but no way was she leaving without her brother, so she reluctantly gave in.

They searched quietly among some boxes but found nothing for what they were looking. Buddy was about to call the search off when Cally noticed a large bag that was partially hidden behind a blanket, suspended on a hanger from a water pipe in one of the ceiling joists. It was the kind of bag that clothes were put in from the dry cleaners, and it was hanging in one of the basement corners. They went to the bag and partially unzipped it. They reached inside it and felt that the material was furry. Yes, there were two ape-like arms attached to the material. It had to be the gorilla suit that Hector Chillblaines had mentioned.

While Buddy was examining the gorilla suit, Cally noticed something hanging up behind it which had been completely hidden by another blanket. She pulled the blanket aside and saw a peculiar-looking mannequin of a woman dressed in what looked like a white wedding gown. "What do you make of this getup, Bud?" she asked her brother quietly.

"Huh? What've you got there?" Buddy looked up from the gorilla suit and eyed the mannequin.

"It's some kind of a big doll dressed in white, the kind that's displayed in stores," Cally replied, not remembering the word "mannequin."

Buddy's eyes lit up as if one hundred-watt light bulbs were shining behind them. "I think we're on to something, Cal!"

"What do you mean?" his sister inquired as she glanced from the gorilla suit to the mannequin and back again.

"Well, some of the guys have reportedly seen a creature that looks like a Bigfoot, remember? This gorilla suit could explain that. And there's a ghost legend that's been around for years claiming that a girl drowned in Moose Lake, and that sometimes her supposed ghost is seen floating about on the surface of the water. That mannequin in the white dress could explain the sightings of the ghost girl out on the lake. Especially if search lights were shined upon the mannequin at night," Buddy added, pointing to several such lights laying on the basement floor in the corner by the gorilla suit and the mannequin.

Suddenly the basement door opened, and the lights came on.

"Let's get out of here quickly!" Buddy ordered.

They sprinted toward the far door. A voice screeched from the top of the stairs, "Who's down here in the basement?" A slender form descended the basement stairs and reached the floor at the same time that Buddy and Cally reached the far door.

They opened it and burst through in almost one motion.

"Where do we go, Bud?" Cally's voice had a tone of panic in it.

Buddy felt panic begin to overwhelm him too, but he fought it down. He quickly scanned their surroundings. On a small knoll just ahead of them, he noticed a little graveyard containing just three headstones. "Let's hide behind the gravestones," he beckoned, grabbing Cally's hand and pulling her in that direction.

They reached the headstones and hunkered down behind two of them just as they heard the basement door open. Neither of the kids moved a muscle for what seemed like an hour though it was only about five minutes. Then they heard the person go back into the basement, and they relaxed from a squatting position to a sitting one with their backs propped against the headstones.

"Whew, that was close!" Buddy whispered, exhaling through clenched teeth.

"Do you think it's safe for us to leave this place?" Cally asked with fear still showing in her eyes.

"I don't know, Cal. It might be better to wait until it gets dark. Then we'd be sure the Chillblaines couldn't spot us."

"Wait until dark? That's at least a few hours from now. I don't know if I can stay here that long, Bud."

But the Chambers kids didn't have long to wait as things turned out. About ten minutes later, they heard the Chillblaines's car start, and then they saw it winding down the long driveway and enter Highway 27, going out of sight.

"Now that they know somebody was in their house, I wonder where they're going to?" Buddy mused out loud. "Maybe to the police. Well Sis, let's now get out of here!"

As they were about to leave, they turned toward the two gravestones while standing up. What they read on the stones astounded them. On Buddy's stone was the name "Florence Foster, wife of Peter and mother of Stanley." On Cally's stone was the name "Irene Chillblaines, wife of Horace." They then read the third gravestone which had the inscription: "Agnes Chillblaines, wife of Hector."

"So, Stanley said his mom, grandmother, and great-aunt were all killed in a car accident," Buddy said loudly, not worrying anymore about being heard by the Chillblaines. "Florence Foster, wife of Peter, and mother of Stanley is buried here along with these two Chillblaines women, which I guess we can assume are her mother and aunt. If that is correct, then Stanley is related to Horace and Hector Chillblaines!"

Cally was too dumbfounded at first to say anything. She just stared at the inscriptions on the gravestones. Finally, she said, "No wonder the Chillblaines brothers are so bitter! They lost both of their wives and a daughter and niece in one day."

"C'mon, Cal, let's get back to camp," Buddy said, trying to encourage his sister. He knew full well she'd been through a very exhausting day with their mom in the hospital, the episode with the musky fish, the emotionally—draining time on the hike, and now the narrow escape with the Chillblaines, and this possible revelation about Stanley Foster. She had to be drained of strength, for he himself was.

They jogged slowly back to camp, still being cautious about being seen, using trees for cover when available.

They made it back to camp just as the hikers were returning from their hike. Some of the hikers were talking excitedly to one another, something about Stanley Foster not being with them.

Janet spotted the Chambers kids and asked them if Stanley had come back to camp with them. They assured her that he hadn't.

Pastor Randy had now joined up with the group after hearing the commotion from his cabin.

"What's this about Stanley not returning with the other hikers?" he asked Janet with a look of concern upon his face.

"Well Roger said he went back to get his hiking stick, but he never returned to the main group," Janet replied. "The strange thing is that when we got back to the place in the trail where Stanley left Roger, we found his hiking stick propped up against a tree where he'd left it. He never did get his stick."

"Maybe he saw some interesting wildlife and wanted a closer look," Pastor Randy said though he was not really convinced. "Let's wait a little longer and see if he comes in on his own." He looked around the group. And by the expressions on their faces, he could tell that they believed Stanley was lost in the woods. "Anyway," he added trying to be cheerful for the campers, "it's right about in the middle of swim time. How about we all go for a quick dip before supper?"

Nobody wanted to even though it was a hot afternoon.

"Pastor Randy," Buddy spoke up. "May I talk with you privately? Cally and I have discovered a few things about the Chillblaines brothers."

"Huh? Oh, sure," Pastor Randy replied, taken a little by surprise at Buddy's remark.

Buddy, Cally, and Pastor Randy strolled back to the latter's cabin for a little discussion on the topic at hand. The rest of the campers just wandered around as if they were in a daze.

*****

Stanley at first felt that he was in no danger. All he had to do was backtrack his way until he found the trail and then head back to camp. He had already had enough of this day's hike, and he didn't want to even find the rest of the hikers. Instead, he wanted only to go back to his cabin and take a good long nap.

But he had left no tracks on the forest floor to follow back to the trail. And when minutes of searching for it turned into an hour, Stanley did become anxious. Another half hour of searching unsuccessfully for the trail brought panic to the boy. He ran and ran, tripping over branches, falling through bramble bushes, and yelling out the word "help!" over and over until he became hoarse. And of course, no one came to help him.

He sat on a stump. His heart raced from fear and exertion. He breathed in long deep breaths, calming himself so that he could think more clearly. What should he do? He had been a couple of years in the Boy Scouts, and he remembered the leaders telling him that if he ever got lost, to stay put until help arrived. That seemed like the most reasonable thing to do at the moment, so he stayed put.

Not only did he feel scared, he felt really vulnerable right now. It was a new, strange feeling too because in all of his life, Stanley Foster had never felt vulnerable before. At times, now he felt like crying, but he blinked back the tears, trying to stay in control.

Control. Yes, that's what he had always tried to maintain in his life. He had always wanted to be the master not the servant. To be someone's servant, he believed, was to be weak. And Stanley didn't want to be weak. The only thing now was that he did feel weak, and he wasn't anyone's servant either. He knew he needed help, and he needed it soon too.

"So, I guess being a servant isn't being weak," he spoke out loud as the thought struck him. "Those who hopefully will be looking for me will be my servants, and those guys will be heroes."

He glanced upward at the sun to see how late in the day it was getting to be. He realized he had several hours yet before dark. But what if no one found him by dark? He would need shelter from the elements and from possible rogue animals that could attack him then. He shuddered at that thought. He was also starting to get hungry.

He began to get panicked again because he knew he had to make a decision soon. But if he made the wrong one, he could be in big trouble.

"Think, Stanley, think!" he scolded himself as he struck his head several times with his hand. "Okay, guy, reason it out. The Boy Scouts recommend staying put until someone finds you. But on the other hand, if no one does find me, and soon it's going to get dark, really dark. And I don't want a ferocious bear running into me at night. Also, it could rain, or at the least some dew could get me wet, so I'll need shelter from the elements. Maybe I could find a cave or something. But what if after I'd leave here someone would come right to this very spot? That would be just my luck! Nothing ever goes my way anyway. Probably nobody will even find me. It's very possible that I'll be lost out here until I starve to death." Stanley was now starting to feel sorry for himself. "It's almost like God has cursed my life!"

This last thought jolted him back to reality. An image of God seated on His throne came to him.

"Pray, Stanley, pray!" a voice seemed to say to him in his mind.

He sat up straight and scanned the heavens. Had someone up there just spoken to him? *It must be my imagination,* he thought. But the impression of the words persisted.

"Pray, Stanley!"

"I've never prayed before in my life! Oh, Dad has prayed with me at mealtimes and before bed, but I've never actually prayed personally. I don't even really know how."

He was amazed that he was speaking out loud. But to whom? He convinced himself that he was just talking to no one in particular. Still the impression stayed with him.

Perhaps it was the uncomfortable feeling that Stanley got from thinking these thoughts. Maybe he really didn't believe what the Boy Scouts had taught him. In any event, he left the area slowly at first as if he hadn't fully made up his mind. But then, his pace quickened until he was almost jogging. It didn't matter to him where he was going. He was lost and direction was irrelevant. The thing he wanted and looked for was shelter. Maybe he could find a cave to rest in, to protect him from wild animals, the weather, and unconsciously from these thoughts and feelings that he was having.

Stanley skirted a clump of blue-spruce trees, and then descended into a valley where a white rippled stream was flowing. He had also learned that if you follow a stream down its course, you should eventually come out to some sort of civilization.

But he crossed the stream on some rocks instead because he didn't know how far he'd have to go downstream to find a cabin or house.

A ruffed grouse burst out of a thicket near the stream and winged its way in a blur of feathers into a tangled mass of vines and underbrush some distance away.

The "explosion" of the bird as it shot into the sky scared Stanley so badly that he almost fell to his knees.

God must really want me to pray! The thought crossed his mind like lightning as he caught himself from falling down.

Regaining his composure, he climbed the far side of the valley he'd just come down, puffing from the exertion. He stopped on the top of the hill, wheezing until he caught his breath. Then he set out again for destinations unknown.

*****

Pastor Randy was on the phone, talking to Sheriff Greene from Northridge.

"Yes, sir, that's right," Pastor Randy confirmed to the sheriff the information he'd just given to him. "Yes, sir, the missing boy's name is Stanley Foster. He's about thirteen years old, I believe. He was supposed to return with the other hikers from a trip they'd taken, but he didn't. I'm afraid he's lost out there in the woods, and night will be here soon."

Pastor Randy listened for several seconds then continued. "I've already contacted his dad. He doesn't have a mother. She died several years ago. At least that's the information I got when he registered for camp."

Pause.

"So, you'll be sending out a team of the search and rescue unit. That's great, sir. Uh, by the way, do you mind if some of the campers go out looking for him? It won't be until morning of course. And I will personally lead them in the search. I think it would be better than them sitting around, moping about Stanley."

Pause.

"Thank you, sir!" Pastor Randy hung up the phone and then headed for the cafeteria. It was just about supper time, and he wanted to make an announcement to the campers.

As he entered the cafeteria, he noticed that most of the campers were there, but they weren't in their usual joyous mood. Some of them were sitting by themselves with their heads tilted forward, resting on their hands. Others were in little groups, talking quietly among themselves.

It seemed strange to Pastor Randy that many of the kids who did not seem to like Stanley were now actually worried for his safety. *Well, that's good!* he thought to himself. *I'm glad to see some concern for others.*

He cleared his throat then called for everyone's attention. "I've just gotten off the phone with Sheriff Greene of Northridge. He's given us permission to go out as a group tomorrow morning to help hunt for Stanley. Does anyone want to go?"

Several gloomy faces brightened at his suggestion. Hands went up from all over the room, and some of the campers became excited over the possibility of them helping to find Stanley.

"Great!" Pastor Randy exclaimed. "Let's meet here in front of the cafeteria at seven tomorrow morning. Now let's get some supper before we all faint from hunger. Then we wouldn't be of any use to Stanley."

After they had eaten and prayed for Stanley, Pastor Randy dismissed the group directly to their cabins. Under the circumstances, he felt it was better to cancel the evening activities and service to allow the campers to have personal time for reflection and prayer for Stanley and for themselves. At such a serious time as this, he knew that it was a "perfect" opportunity for them to settle issues with the Lord. And it wouldn't hurt them to get a little more "shut-eye" than usual. Tomorrow would be a physical and emotional challenge for everyone.

On their way back to their cabins, Buddy and Cally discussed the situation about Stanley.

"I've got mixed emotions about this whole thing with Stanley," Buddy confessed. "Part of me is really sorry that he's lost, and that he's probably terrified in the woods. But part of me feels like he deserves what he is going through for the miserable way that he's acted toward us."

"I know, I feel the same way," Cally replied, actually relieved that she finally got her feelings out. "But I have to keep reminding myself that Stanley acts miserable because he probably feels miserable on the inside."

"Well, despite my less than noble feelings for Stanley, I'm going to try to help find him tomorrow," Buddy said with determination.

"Me too," Cally said with equal determination.

At this point, the path split to the cabins so the Chambers kids went their separate ways to retire for the night.

CHAPTER 6

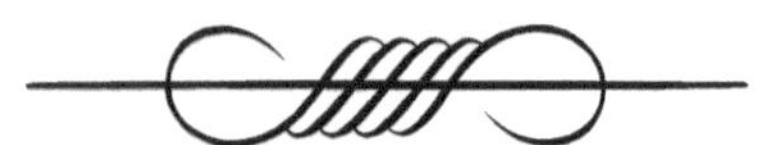

Horace and Hector Chillblaines had driven to the sheriff's department to report the break-in at their home. Now they were talking to Sheriff Greene in his office about the situation.

"That's right, Sheriff, some people, and I saw two going out of the basement, had been in our house, snooping around when we caught them. Or rather, we almost caught them. They actually got away!" Horace was recalling the scene in his mind, and he emphasized what he reported by waving his arms back and forth.

Hector agreed with everything his brother said and showed it by nodding his head vigorously.

"Well did you get a good look at the two?" Sheriff Greene asked, looking from Horace to Hector.

"Not exactly," Horace replied. "But we know they probably were from Camp Musky because they looked like young people and that camp is in operation now."

"We'll have to contact the camp," Sheriff Greene replied. "By the way, do you keep your doors locked?"

Horace and Hector both looked up in surprise.

"No," Horace replied slowly and sheepishly.

"Well, besides the situation we're talking about of a break-in, I've read in today's paper that there's been some strange tracks spotted at Camp Musky," Sheriff Greene said. "Says it might be Bigfoot tracks. Now I don't believe in a Bigfoot, but until the situation is cleared up, you may want to lock your doors. You never know what you might find in your house."

Horace and Hector glanced at each other. "Yeah, Sheriff, I guess you're right," Horace said with narrowed eyes.

"Anyway" Sheriff Greene cautioned, "keep your eyes peeled for anyone or anything that comes around your home."

*****

With the first hint of light the next morning, George and Fred woke from a restless night of attempted sleep in these Northwoods. The mosquitoes had been very annoying, and the dampness of the night had added greatly to their discomfort. George had propped his back against a tree because he hadn't wanted to lay on the chilly, damp ground. The problem was every time he began to nod off to sleep, his head would droop forward, causing a reflex action in his neck muscles to jerk his head upwards. Each time he did this, he whacked the back of his head against the tree.

Fred, who was in pain from his broken bones, had no choice but to lay on the ground. Now he was so stiff that he could barely move. He rubbed his head and felt that his hair was as matted down as the moss and leaves that he had rested upon.

"Man, oh man, am I sore," Fred moaned. "I feel like I've been hit by a truck!"

George's eyes popped wide open at the sound of the word "truck." "I just remembered," he exclaimed. "We've got to find the truck, so we can get out of here! I don't want to spend another night in this wilderness!"

Fred groaned as he struggled to sit up. "Well, you're on your own, man. I can't help you find the truck." He managed to prop his back against a tree while holding his rib cage and wincing from the pain.

"All right," George said with a grim look on his face. "I guess it's up to me to get us out of here! I know we're lost, I mean like totally lost. But never fear! George is here!"

He squinted his eyes, jumped to his feet, and lunged through the wall of evergreen trees that they had used to protect them from the wind.

"Hey, Fred," George said in an embarrassed tone of voice.

"What?" Fred asked, rather annoyed.

"The truck was only twenty feet from us all last night!"

*****

Buddy and Cally both were up early with the rest of the campers. They all met outside the cafeteria as Pastor Randy had told them to last evening. Pete Foster, Stanley's dad, had already joined up with the group. The youth pastor then instructed the group, "We're all going out to look for Stanley as you know," he began. "Please stay together as a group. We don't want any of you getting lost! Also, within our group, I want each of you to pair off with someone for double security. All right, now find a partner."

Buddy and Cally formed a pair as did all the rest of the campers in the group. When Pastor Randy was satisfied with the pairing, he led the group in a prayer and then they set out in search of Stanley. The first ten minutes of the search was fun for everyone. But after that it began to be real work, climbing up and down hills, forcing one's self through brush, and leaping over fallen trees was taking its toll on the group.

Overhead, the group saw a helicopter with the words "Search and Rescue" written on the sides. Several times, they caught a glimpse through the trees of a contingent of searchers, wearing orange vests, combing the hillsides. Hopefully Stanley would be found soon. But as they all would learn later, this was not to be the case.

*****

Stanley had wandered for hours, and the sun was now getting close to the horizon in the west. Strangely his having walked apparently for miles had had a calming effect upon him. He was able to think much more clearly than before. And he no longer was afraid. He decided to try giving prayer a chance.

"Lord," he began slowly, "I know I've been a bad guy all of my life. But I feel You want me to pray to You. Anyway, if You're really here, I ask that You would protect me, and that someone would find me soon. Thank You, amen." He felt a relief surge through him. Stanley now sensed that everything would be all right.

As he opened his eyes, he saw what appeared to be a windfall up ahead. Curious, he strode over to it and found a large tree which had been blown over by the wind. Underneath its root system was a large hollowed-out place in the soil. He could see that no animals were in it, so he decided to climb down into the depression. Stanley found that he could lie down in the hole without touching either side with his head or feet. This was great!

He always carried a Swiss Army knife with him, and he now took it out of his pocket. He opened the saw blade on it, then went into the woods, and cut a number of spruce boughs. These he dragged back to the hole in the windfall and lined the dirt floor with them. Now he would have a soft bed on which to sleep. He went back to the spruces and cut one more bough with which he would use to cover himself as a blanket when he slept.

Darkness was now coming on, so Stanley retired for the night, snuggling down in his spruce bed and savored the "piney" scent which it exuded. He knew that he needed to cover the windfall with a spruce-bough roof to keep out any rain. That, however, would have to wait until tomorrow when he had daylight in which to do it in.

Stanley was very hungry. But finding something to eat would also have to wait until tomorrow. He settled in upon his newly made bed, covered himself with the spruce bough, and fell into a deep sleep.

*****

Next morning, as the sun shone its warming rays upon him, Stanley roused himself from his makeshift home and looked for some breakfast. Though he didn't know it at the time, this was the same morning that the search parties had begun looking for him.

He didn't have far to go to find some delicious food. Ascending a little hill, he saw acres of ripe black berries on the other side. Stanley ate as much as he could hold, then went to a sparkling stream nearby, and drank until his thirst was gone.

Next, he came back to the windfall and spent the next few hours covering it with spruce boughs for protection from the elements. With that accomplished, he nestled into his snug "home" and waited for his rescue.

*****

"Mayday! Mayday!" Jack Mason, the helicopter pilot screamed over his intercom as the "chopper" rolled over to one side, righted itself, and then crashed into the forest below.

The sheriff's office in Northridge picked up the pilot's message over its intercom.

Then silence.

Lucy Wilson, the dispatcher on duty, radioed Sheriff Greene who was in charge of the rescue mission for Stanley Foster. At the moment though, he was taking care of other urgent business, and he had just heard the pilot's call over his own squad car's CB.

"Yeah, that's right, Lucy," Sheriff Greene confirmed. "I heard Jack's 'mayday' just a couple of minutes ago. I'm on it right now. Thanks!"

The squad car's siren blared out its warning as Sheriff Greene sped to Camp Musky. He swerved the car into the gravel lane leading to the camp almost sliding off into the ditch. He skidded to a stop beneath the musky sign, shutting off the motor and the siren almost simultaneously.

Even before the cloud of dust had a chance to settle, he was out of the squad car and pounding on the door of the registration building.

No answer.

He jogged to the cafeteria and pounded on its door.

No answer.

He hurried to the shore of the lake, but no one was around.

"I guess they're all our looking for the kid," he mused to himself.

Sheriff Greene was about to get back into the squad car when he saw a pickup truck rolling up the dusty lane. He watched it pull in beside the squad car. Inside the truck was George Nutter who rolled his window down.

"Howdy, Sheriff," George said. "I've been lookin' for you. I took my buddy, Fred to the Northridge hospital to get his ribs taken care of, and then I went to the station, but Lucy said you were comin' out here to the camp."

"Oh?" Sheriff Greene shoved his hat farther back on his head and leaned against the pickup's cab, "What happened to Fred?"

"That's a long story, Sheriff," George replied sheepishly. "What I wanted to see you about though is if I could join in the rescue of the downed chopper pilot? Fred and I heard about it on our radio."

"Yeah, you can join in the search. I was about to get started myself," Sheriff Greene said. "Let's see. East is over that way," the sheriff pointed with his finger in the proper direction. "I hope we can reach the pilot in time."

Sheriff Greene radioed to his deputy, Don Phillips, who was leading the main rescue effort for Stanley. "Hey, Don, how's it going with the search team?"

"Okay, I guess," Don replied. "We haven't seen any signs of the Foster boy though. Hey, Sheriff, have you heard any more about Jack Mason's situation?"

"Not yet," Sheriff Greene replied. "George Nutter and I are about to look for him. I know he was a little too inexperienced to be flying that chopper, but we had no choice. He was the only man available. Anyhow, Don, I would like for you to take the boys and wait for us to reach you all. When George and I rendezvous with you, we'll take turns carrying Jack, or Jack's body, down to the camp."

"That's a big ten-four," Don responded, trying to sound official. "We're just now on the site of that old abandoned logging area about a quarter mile west of camp. Oh, and by the way, Sheriff, I had reported the crash to headquarters just after Lucy had called you apparently. That's why I didn't call you about it personally," Don lied.

"Okay, Don. We'll be up to you shortly. Over and out." Sheriff Greene rolled his eyes. *That's just like Don,* he thought to himself as he wrestled the sturdy plastic stretcher from the squad car. *He's always lying to cover for himself so that he won't get into trouble.*

The fact that Don and the boys had only covered a quarter of a mile from Camp Musky was probably due to them taking a nap when the crash occurred. Too many donuts on the job didn't help the situation either. They probably only learned of the crash after Lucy had radioed them.

Sheriff Greene and George each carried an end of the stretcher upon which the men would transport Jack. Then they headed to the logging site to meet up with Don and the others.

*****

Pastor Randy, who had teamed up with Pete Foster, called for the campers to take a break, "Let's rest awhile, guys," he said, puffing for air while the sweat streamed down his forehead. Everyone dropped to the ground instantly.

"While we're resting, let's pray for Jack Mason," he urged the group. They bowed their heads while Pastor Randy led them in a prayer for Jack and also for Stanley.

The campers had seen the helicopter go down. But since they were too far away to help Jack and didn't have CBs, they had only watched in horror. A short time later, however, they had heard the distant wail of a siren, and they had hoped and prayed that help would be coming for Jack soon.

Pastor Randy knew that he couldn't have the campers searching all day for Stanley. They were already getting tired, and they would have to return to camp before it got dark, or else they might become lost. So, after their break, he decided to call off the search and have everyone return the way they had come. It wouldn't be hard finding their way back because the bushes and other vegetation they had walked through were somewhat crushed by the campers.

He also knew there was nothing that they could do for Jack except pray. The helicopter he had been flying was the only one that Northridge had. He had heard on the news that the nearest city with more choppers, Collinsville, was using those to help put out wildfires, some four to five hours away. So there likely wouldn't be any more search and rescue in the air for Stanley. It would all have to be done on foot and that was going to take time.

*****

Sheriff Greene and George Nutter soon met up with Deputy Don Phillips and some of the other search and rescue team members. Don had split the main group into two teams so that they could cover more territory. The real reason for the split, Sheriff Greene suspected, was so that Don and his cronies could lag behind the others, letting team B do most of the work. Then when Stanley was found, Don would take all the credit as the leader of the search effort.

"You boys enjoying the shade?" Sheriff Greene asked with a smirk as he glanced at Deputy Phillips and company sprawled out beneath some trees.

Deputy Phillips sat up quickly, trying to regain his composure. "Well, Sheriff, we were just waitin' for you two to arrive just like you told us to."

"Oh, okay, now we're here. A couple of you boys take this stretcher for a while. George and I need a little breather," Sheriff

Greene spoke as he and George handed the stretcher to four receptive hands. "Let's head east and try to find Jack."

The men, now eight in number, began the hike in search of the chopper. Sheriff Greene thought it was good that no smoke was coming from the crash site. It would have made finding Jack easier, but at least there were no fires with which they had to be concerned.

About two hours later, the searchers came to a rugged part of the country—wilderness actually—and found the wreckage of the chopper. It was lying in a small canyon about fifty feet down.

"No wonder Jack crashed," Sheriff Greene realized out loud. "Winds coming from this little canyon could wreak havoc upon a chopper. That plus all the tall trees here would make flying treacherous."

Sheriff Greene thought about calling out to Jack but then decided against it.

The men secured ropes to some trees on the edge of the canyon, then climbed slowly down to the bottom. They carefully made their way over the debris, finally coming to the chopper's cockpit.

Even before the men looked inside, they heard Jack moan softly.

"Thank God, he's still alive!" Sheriff Greene exclaimed.

Slowly, ever so slowly, the eight rescuers released the unconscious man from the pilot's seat and strapped him onto the stretcher. Then they began the arduous process of transporting him back up the canyon and then to Camp Musky.

*****

Hector and Horace Chillblaines were watching the midday news. A reporter was telling the story of the downed chopper and also of the search and rescue attempt to find Stanley Foster.

"So, the boy got himself lost in the woods, did he?" Horace chuckled at the news report. "Serves the brat right."

The Chillblaines brothers listened with fascination to each detail of the story.

Finally, Horace spoke again. "You know Hector, this newscast gives me a great idea. It looks like everyone is gone from the camp right now. Why don't you and I make the campsite a visit? We could really do the place some damage and make sure that nobody ever comes back to camp again!" He snickered at the thought.

Hector squinted his eyes a few moments and replied in his squeaky voice. "Why do we have to go to the trouble of all that? We already own the property these people use for going to camp. With the lease up this year, they won't be able to go to camp anyway."

"They won't be able to use our land, that's all!" Horace emphasized this fact to his brother. "They could still come to the camp and use the buildings which the camp owns. Some sympathetic judge might just let them use part of our land around the buildings. Anyway, I want to make sure that no one ever comes back to any of these premises!" he pounded his hand on his palm as he spoke. "If the buildings aren't being used, chances are they'll sell them to us. I wish I'd never allowed those buildings to be built in the first place."

"Won't the campers blame the wreckage on us since we're the only ones who live around here?" Hector inquired.

"Not if we make them think an animal did it," Horace chuckled. "Maybe something like a Bigfoot." He clapped his hands together in delight. "They'll be so scared that none of them will ever come back!"

Hector finally agreed to be a part of the mayhem at Camp Musky. The two brothers decided to bring along homemade devices which strapped to their feet, producing "Bigfoot" tracks. They also took along baseball bats for doing the real damage.

When they got to Camp Musky, Horace fitted the truck-makers onto his feet and began producing tracks in the soft earth. Both men broke windows and other things with the baseball bats. They wore gloves so as not to leave fingerprints.

Fifteen minutes of destruction was all that the brothers needed to complete their mission. They made sure that food items were strewn about as if a hungry animal had been to blame for the mess. When the breakage was satisfactory to the Chillblaines, Horace removed the track-makers and then smugly remarked, "That ought to keep those pesky campers from ever coming back to these buildings!" Hector nodded his approval, and the two men left.

*****

It was about 3:00 p.m. when Pastor Randy and Pete Foster brought the campers back to camp. The shock that each one experienced at the sight of the wreckage was incredible. Buddy noticed the large tracks in the earth almost at once. "Hey, Pastor Randy, come and take a look at this," he exclaimed as he stooped to examine the tracks.

"Well, well," the youth pastor remarked.

"What do you make of these tracks, Buddy?"

By now, Cally and the others hurried over to see the tracks.

"What made these big tracks?" Clarence asked with big eyes.

"I have my suspicions," Buddy replied. "I also have my suspicions who did all this damage too."

While the campers were busy examining the tracks and looking at the damage done to the buildings, Buddy and Cally privately talked with Pastor Randy.

"Yeah, I remember you guys telling me about the gorilla suit you both saw in the Chillblaines's basement," Pastor Randy said, rubbing his chin with his fingers. "But we have to get absolute proof that the Chillblaines made these tracks. We can't go on suspicion."

"I have an idea," Buddy said thoughtfully, a sly grin developing on his face. "I'll examine these tracks to see if there are any peculiar marks on them. Then I'll try to sneak back into the Chillblaines's basement and see if their track-making thingies have the same mark or marks on them. We'll know for sure if the Chillblaines did make the tracks."

"That's a good plan, but it's awfully risky," Pastor Randy cautioned. "You could get into a lot of trouble for trespassing."

"That's if I get caught," Buddy replied. "I'm not planning on getting caught."

"I want to go with you, Buddy," his sister pleaded.

"No, Cal, not this time. I could get into the house and out more easily if I was alone. The Chillblaines will probably be more on their guard now."

Pastor Randy and Cally agreed reluctantly to Buddy's plan. The youth pastor later gave him one of his walkie-talkies just in case he got into trouble. Now all Buddy had to do was wait for the right time to find those tracking devices.

*****

Sheriff Greene and company arrived at Camp Musky around 5:00 p.m. He had already called in for an ambulance to be waiting for them. By now, Jack Mason was semiconscious, drifting in and out of consciousness. The EMTs transferred him from the stretcher to a gurney lified him into the ambulance, and drove him to the Northridge hospital.

The sheriff's attention was now directed toward the destruction done to the camp buildings. "It looks like a tornado hit this place," he commented with great concern. He asked around if anyone had seen what had happened. Pastor Randy said he thought that the Chillblaines brothers might have done it, but he wasn't sure.

Sheriff Greene dismissed this proposition at once as being preposterous. He then went to his squad car and retrieved some instruments with which to do detective work.

The sheriff and his deputy dusted down the place for prints. They found many but wouldn't know whose they were until they took the prints to the lab in Northridge.

After Sheriff Greene had finished the investigation, he and his men had supper with the campers. Even though the cooks had been on the search for Stanley with the rest of the group, they had returned in time to fix a quick supper.

Since it was now late in the day, the sheriff and his deputy went back to Northridge after eating. The other men in search team A also went home as did those in team B about an hour later, coming in from the forest.

After supper, Pastor Randy had the campers cut cardboard boxes into sizes which fit the broken windows, then had these pieces of cardboard duct-taped into place.

"That's about all we can do this evening," the youth pastor explained to the group. "Tomorrow we can clean up more of the mess. Let's have a quick devotion before you all go back to the cabins for the night." A few minutes later, all the campers went back to their respective cabins. All that is except one. Buddy stayed behind.

*****

Buddy waited until midnight before venturing forth to the Chillblaines's mansion. A crescent moon spilled a little silver light upon the countryside, giving Buddy just enough sight to see where he was going. It wasn't long before he had reached the mansion.

Buddy hoped that the Chillblaines had put the track makers back into the basement. He tried the basement door, and to his surprise, it opened. Apparently, the Chillblaines hadn't learned their lesson from the last time or perhaps they wanted to set a trap. That last thought bothered him.

He shined the flashlight he had brought with him for this purpose. Snooping around, Buddy found the track-makers on the floor just beneath the gorilla suit. He turned the fake feet over and examined the bottom of each one. Sure enough, the markings on these devices appeared to match the markings in the soil prints near the camp buildings. This was the evidence for which he was looking.

Buddy shined his light on the mannequin that he and Cally had seen the previous time. *The Chillblaines are sure predictable people. This thing and the gorilla suit are in the exact spot they were a few days ago*, he thought.

Or maybe he was the one who was a little too predictable. He heard a sound above him, and the lights in the basement flashed on. Someone was coming down the stairway.

Buddy turned to run out the basement door. It opened. Someone was coming in that door.

Horace and Hector Chillblaines had him trapped between them. The two men closed in upon him. Horace grabbed him from behind, and Hector seized him from the front.

Buddy quickly retrieved the walkie-talkie from his pocket and blurted into it, "Pastor Randy, help!"

*****

Stanley was truly enjoying his stay in the wilderness. He had plenty to eat and drink, as well as a cozy little dwelling in which to stay. Just now, he was asleep within the windfall. Several hours before, he had looked up through his spruce-bough roof to enjoy the stars and the crescent moon. He had even identified a few of the constellations he had learned in Boy Scouts: Orion with his three-star belt; Arcturus, the Bear; and the Pleiades, the seven sisters.

Stanley had been so enthralled at the heavenly light show that he had found himself speaking out loud, "Thank You, Lord!"

CHAPTER 7

Pastor Randy heard the frantic call from Buddy at 1:00 a.m. He fell out of bed in his rush to get up and stubbed his toe twice in his hurry to get dressed. Taking his flashlight, he jogged down the lane leading to the Chillblaines's home.

When he got there, he paused for a few seconds on the front porch, gaining some courage. Seeing that lights were still on inside the mansion, he knocked.

A few seconds later, Horace opened the door and smiled a perfectly evil smile at the youth pastor. He spoke first, "Why, hello, uh, Pastor Randy Brewer, I believe."

"Yes, that's who I am. Mr. Chillblaines, I'll get right to the point. I'm here to get Buddy Chambers."

"Buddy Chambers?" Horace repeated the name rather sarcastically. "There's no Buddy Chambers here. In fact, nobody has been to our house all day," he lied.

"Well, I received a distress call from Buddy not more than twenty minutes ago and"—Pastor Randy caught himself. If he admitted that Buddy had been here, he would be admitting that the boy had trespassed on the Chillblaines's property.

Horace knew he had the advantage. He grinned condescendingly at the youth pastor. "That distress call could have come from anywhere. Perhaps the boy got lost in the woods."

"Well, all the distress call said was, 'Pastor Randy, help!' If Buddy had been in the woods, he would have told me his relative location. The call sounded more like he was being held captive, and he didn't have enough time to tell me more."

"Perhaps the boy's walkie-talkie batteries went dead, and he couldn't transmit anything further." Horace grinned. "Or perhaps he fell over a cliff and became unconscious. Any number of things could have happened to the Chambers boy. All I know is that he isn't here. If I were you, pastor, I would be looking for him elsewhere. It sounds like he might really be in trouble." Horace's grin turned into a scowl.

Pastor Randy knew he was defeated for the time being. He'd have to come up with a quick plan to try to rescue Buddy though. He went back to his cabin to think and pray.

*****

Horace and Hector had hog-tied Buddy and gagged his mouth with a handkerchief tied around his head. He was sitting against a block wall in the basement when the brothers came down to him again.

"What are we going to do with the boy," Hector asked his brother nervously.

"Well, we can't let him go so that he can blab what we've done to him and Camp Musky's property, that's for sure," Horace responded. "I think there's only one thing we can do."

"You don't mean"—Hector stopped in midsentence and looked at Horace with a shudder of horror running up his spine.

"He's already tied and gagged," Horace commented, gesturing with a bony finger at Buddy. "We could take him out onto Moose Lake with our rowboat and dump him into the water."

"That'd be m-m-murder!" Hector choked out that last word.

"Nobody'd ever find the body because we'd weigh him down with a cinder block," Horace tried to reassure his brother.

"They could always dredge the lake," Hector said, trying to convince his sibling.

"Oh, stop fretting," Horace commanded. "It's really the only way we could get rid of the body. If we dug a grave, a police dog would most likely find it."

Buddy had been listening to this conversation, and now he realized just how dangerous these two brothers could be. It was true that Hector had more of a conscience than Horace, but he was too weak to stand up to his brother. Horace would win out in the end, and Hector would go along with him. That made the weak-willed one just as guilty though as the strong-willed one. Buddy prayed silently.

The Chillblaines brothers untied Buddy's feet and ungagged him but left his hands tied behind his back. They pulled him to his feet.

"You're coming with us, boy!" Horace ordered roughly.

Buddy didn't struggle with them. He needed all of his strength and mental abilities to try to escape this plight. Like Stanley, he had been in the Boy Scouts, and he liked to carry a pocket knife with him when at camp. If he could just get to it!

The three left the house through the basement door. They brought along a cinder block which the brothers carried between them. They took the most direct route to Moose Lake which led them through thick bushes and other vegetation. Buddy didn't feel the scratches on him that he would notice later.

When the three reached the edge of the lake, the Chillblaines uncovered a rowboat that had been hidden under a camouflaged tarp. Horace and Hector then directed Buddy onto the back seat of the boat. The two brothers set the cinder block down in the bottom of the boat and sat on the seat in the middle. Each one took an oar with which to row.

Buddy didn't want to die of course. But he was not afraid to die. Last summer at Camp Musky, he had given his life to Christ, and he was now trusting Him as Savior and Lord. Knowing his salvation was secure, he tried to reason with the brothers. "If you kill me, they'll put you both into prison for the rest of your lives, you know that, don't you?"

Horace snarled. "Shut up. They won't find you anyway."

"You're wrong about that," Buddy replied. "I agree with your brother that they'll dredge the lake and find my body. The lake is pretty big but not that big. And when they find my body, they'll be able to piece the evidence together and convict you both."

Hector stopped rowing and slumped his head forward. Apparently, he was having second thoughts. He even hung one of his legs over the side of the boat, dragging it in the water as if trying to stop the craft. Suddenly he yelled. "Something grabbed onto my foot!" Hector pulled his leg out of the water with such force that he rocked the boat sharply. Horace lost his balance and plunged into the lake. The boat then rocked steeply the other way, and Hector flipped into the lake. Buddy was sitting in the center of his seat, and therefore, he wasn't moved like the Chillblaines had been. With Hector out of the boat, the craft came back to a more stable position, only slightly swaying from side to side.

The rowboat wasn't more than one hundred yards out on the lake when this incident occurred. Buddy quickly laid on his stomach in the boat with his legs floating on the water behind it. Then he kicked his legs furiously, driving the boat forward until he had reached shore. The lake bottom was shallow enough at this point for Buddy to walk in. This he did, coming out onto the land.

He ran as fast as he could for the lane leading back to camp. It was hard going at first. He had to thrash through the willow clumps and other lakeside growth. But the moon once again gave him just enough light to see where he was going.

He reached the lane and sprinted to find Pastor Randy. Behind him, he could hear the brothers splashing in the lake and arguing about whose fault this had been.

When he reached the youth pastor's cabin, Buddy banged upon the cabin door with his forehead. Pastor Randy, who had been praying the whole time since leaving the Chillblaines's place, quickly arose from his knees and opened the door.

"Pastor Randy, help!" Buddy spoke the exact words which the youth pastor had heard him speak over the walkie-talkie an hour earlier.

"What on earth happened to you, Buddy!" Pastor Randy examined the boy who was dripping wet, plastered with mud, bleeding from scratches on his arms and face, and tied with a rope.

"I'm suffering from a severe case of the Chillblains," Buddy quipped, obviously relieved at being out of his predicament. While Pastor Randy untied the ropes on Buddy's wrists, the boy briefly told the youth pastor what had happened to him in the past two hours.

"They actually tried to murder you?" Pastor Randy asked incredulously.

"Yes," Buddy said in a calm manner, though inwardly, he was still feeling a bit shaky.

"We've got to call the police right now about this situation," Pastor Randy was striding to the phone as he spoke.

*****

The phone rang at 2:15 a.m. in Sheriff Greene's bedroom. The sound brought him out of a deep sleep as he sat straight up in bed. He reached for the receiver, knocked it to the floor, then retrieved it, and brought it to his ear and mouth.

"H-h-hello," he stammered with a yawn.

"Sheriff Greene, this is Randy Brewer at Camp Musky. I'm so sorry to disturb you at this time of night, but what I have to tell you can't wait until morning." Pastor Randy told the Sheriff everything he knew about what the Chillblaines had been up to.

"Attempted murder against Buddy Chambers?" Sheriff Greene couldn't believe his ears. "Uh-huh. Uh-huh. Okay, I'll be down to the camp as soon as I can." Sheriff Greene hung up the phone and quickly got dressed.

*****

The sheriff's squad car pulled up in front of the Chillblaines's mansion at about 3:00 a.m. Sheriff Greene, backed by Deputy Don Phillips, knocked on the same door that Pastor Randy had earlier that night. A light came on inside the house. Soon the door opened a crack and Horace spoke in a rather irritated voice. "Can't a person get some sleep around here? What's the problem, Sheriff?"

"There's been a charge against you and Hector, Sir," Sheriff Greene said, wiping his feet slowly on the welcome mat.

"What's the charge, and who made it?" Horace said defiantly.

"Well, Sir, actually uh. It's an attempted murder charge, and it was reported to us by Pastor Randy Brewer for the kid, Buddy Chambers."

"Well, we haven't seen anyone this evening, especially someone named Buddy Chambers, nor have we been anywhere except in our home," he continued his fabrication. "Now, Sheriff, can I go back to bed? I am literally exhausted."

Horace now was telling the truth. After he and Hector had thrashed their way to Moose Lake's shore, they had stumbled their wearied bodies through the thick brush back to their house. Afterward they had practically dragged themselves to their respective bedrooms and dropped their worn-out selves into their beds.

"I'm afraid we'll have to take you both down to the station in Northridge for an interrogation. You'll have to spend the rest of the night in a jail cell. Tomorrow morning we'll ask you, separately of course, some questions about the attempted murder charge."

The Chillblaines brothers entered the squad car reluctantly. They knew, however, that they had no choice.

After the drive to the police station, Sheriff Greene and his deputy locked the brothers in a jail cell. With that done, they went to their houses and back to bed.

*****

Dave Chambers, Buddy and Cally's dad, was just outside of Northridge when he gave his son a call on his cell phone. "Hey, Buddy, I understand you've had a terrible night. Pastor Randy filled me in on what happened with the Chillblaines brothers. He said Sheriff Greene had everything under control with the brothers going to jail and all, so he decided to call me this morning instead of last night. I can't believe that they actually tried to drown you in the lake."

"That's right, Dad," Buddy replied. "It almost seems funny now with the brothers falling into the lake, but last night, it was pretty freaky."

"Wow, I can imagine," Mr. Chambers said, turning on his left blinker and making a turn into the hospital parking lot. "Thank the Lord you're all right. Hey, Bud, I'm at the hospital to see Mom this morning. I've got to go but keep me posted on how things are going at camp, okay? Love ya."

"Will do, Dad. And tell Mom I love her too," Buddy said and hung up the phone.

Dave Chambers parked his truck, then he made his way to his wife's room in the hospital. Along the way, he reflected about what had happened to his son last night. He had tried to sound calm on the phone so that Buddy wouldn't be more stressed out than he already was. But inside, he was seething with rage at the Chillblaines brothers. Part of his anger was a reaction to the fear that he had about Buddy's narrow escape. He decided not to tell his wife about the incident. She didn't need more stress either.

He entered his wife's room and laid his hand upon her forehead. Linda Chambers opened her eyes and smiled at her husband.

"Hi," she whispered.

He gazed at her with tenderness then spoke with the same emotion. "How are you doing this morning, honey?"

"Oh, I'm still quite sore, but at least I'm sleeping well at night."

"That's good, that's good," Dave said slowly and deliberately for emphasis.

They chitchatted for about a half hour. At one point, Linda told Dave that she thought it was a large black bear that had caused her to crash. Finally, Dave left so as not to wear out his wife. But before leaving, he gave her a kiss and also gave her Buddy's message.

On his way out of the hospital, Dave stopped in to see Jack Mason, the downed helicopter pilot. "Hi, Jack." Dave noticed that his friend was already awake.

"Oh, hi, Dave," Jack said with a look of pleasant surprise.

When Dave asked him how he was feeling, he responded, "I'm feeling much better than yesterday, though my head is still throbbing."

Dave looked at the purple-red spot-on Jack's forehead and spoke. "I'll bet it is! Say, Jack," he continued delicately, "did you get some wind shear in that canyon, causing the chopper to go down?"

"Well," Jack thought for a few moments. "It could have been wind shear that took me down."

"But you're not too sure?" Dave asked, puzzled.

"It's strange," Jack said reminiscing. "It almost felt like something was pulling me down. Now don't laugh at me. It was like a giant grabbed the landing bars on the chopper and yanked me to the ground. I didn't have any control."

A shudder went down Dave's back when he heard Jack's description of the crash. He wondered if what had happened to the chopper could have been from an evil supernatural force—a demonic force? Certainly, there were evil things happening around Camp Musky. The Chillblaines's attempt to murder Buddy was an example of that. "That is strange, Jack. Well, I've got to head to work now. I'll be praying for you."

With that, Dave left the hospital.

*****

Pastor Randy decided not to have the campers go out looking for Stanley anymore. Instead, he let the "professionals" do that job. Pete Foster joined up with them.

Sheriff Greene put Deputy Phillips on another task—that of directing traffic on a road construction project. There he could stand around as much as he wanted to. He appointed one of the men in team B to oversee the search and rescue operation. Sheriff Greene planned on coming again to lead the operation himself when he was able to do so. For now, however, he directed his efforts toward questioning the Chillblaines.

Horace had been placed in interrogation room number one. Hector in interrogation room number two. Horace refused to answer a single question without a lawyer being present. Hector, on the other hand, folded like a tent in a windstorm.

"That's right," Hector said in response to Sheriff Greene's question about Buddy Chambers. "My brother and I took the boy out on the lake last night. Horace actually wanted to drown the boy to keep him silent. I really didn't want to do it, but I couldn't stop him. I tried to stop the boat by sticking my leg in the water, but that didn't help a bit. Something in the water actually bit my foot." He pointed at his shoe with slash marks running the full length of it.

"Something really did a jab on that shoe," Sheriff Greene commented as he stared at Hector's footwear. "Now why did you, or rather Horace, want to keep the Chambers boy quiet?"

"Well, you see," Hector replied a little hesitantly. "Horace and I did a pretty good job of wrecking the camp buildings. That Chambers boy was probably on to us since he was snooping around in our basement. Horace wanted to make sure he didn't talk and ruin our plans of scaring away the campers, so they wouldn't ever come back to this place again."

"Let me get this right," Sheriff Greene said, tapping his pencil on the pad of paper he had been writing on. "Your brother, Horace, would go to the length of murder to silence a boy from talking about damage done to some buildings so that the campers wouldn't come back to Camp Musky?"

Hector waited for several moments before answering. "That's not the whole reason. You see, a few years ago my brother's wife Irene, as well as my wife Agnes, and Horace's daughter Florence Foster were killed in a car crash. Florence of course was Stanley Foster's mother. When she was little, Linda Chambers, Buddy's mother, and Florence were best friends and always were around our places playing together. After the accident, Horace became extremely bitter toward people, life, and especially God. Seeing his grandson, Stanley, growing up without a mother, and seeing young Buddy with his mother, embittered Horace even more. He's turned his bitterness and rage toward Buddy, seeking an excuse to harm him. So, you see, his wanting to drown the boy last night goes much deeper than just keeping him silent."

"That's very interesting," Sheriff Greene said thoughtfully. "Hector, will you sign a statement to what you just told me? And will you testify to all of this in a court of law?"

"Yes, I will," Hector replied, his head bowed in a sense of relief that this whole thing was coming to an end.

*****

Sheriff Greene entered into interrogation room number one and sat down opposite from where Horace Chillblaines was seated at the table. His opinion of both Horace and Hector had changed dramatically.

"So why did you try to drown the Chambers boy last night," he asked, not giving Horace the chance to deny the charge.

Horace was visibly shaken at that comment, realizing that Hector must have "spilled the beans." But then his devious mind thought of a way out of the situation. "That's what the Chambers boy told you, isn't it?" A wicked grin took hold of Horace's wrinkled face, emphasizing the wrinkles even more.

"We have a full written statement by Hector, implicating you in the attempted murder of Buddy Chambers, Sheriff Greene countered.

"If my brother signed a statement of something that he's done, well I'm sure he wanted to ease his conscience. Anything he's told you about me is his word against mine."

"Hector is prepared to witness against you in a court of law. In that case, your fate will be in the hands of a jury," the sheriff warned, pounding a fist upon the table.

Horace's eyes narrowed to a squint. "If he gets a chance to witness that is. I'm not saying another thing without a lawyer being present." He folded his arms in defiance, taking the same stance about not talking as he had upon first entering the interrogation room.

Sheriff Greene knew he was in a "chess game" with Horace, and now they both were at a stalemate. "Go ahead and call your lawyer," he said. "I'll even provide you a quarter."

CHAPTER 8

The fingerprints taken from the crime scene investigation at the camp were negative of course since Horace and Hector Chillblaines had worn gloves so as not to leave any evidence. A technician at the lab called in the results to Sheriff Greene.

"All right, Amy," the sheriff spoke with disappointment. "We'll try to prove their guilt by other means."

Sheriff Greene already had Hector's written statement which would implicate Hector's involvement in the camp's wreckage. That statement, however, might not be enough to convince a jury of Horace's involvement if the case went to court. What they needed was solid proof of his participation as well so that they could nail both of the brothers. But even if such proof could not be found, if both Hector and Buddy testified in court to Horace's attempted murder, that should be enough to put at least Horace away for a long time. Either way though, a case might be made to put Horace or both of the brothers behind prison bars.

He decided to call Pastor Randy for any other clues the youth pastor may have picked up. "This is Sheriff Greene, Pastor. I was wondering if you knew of anything else that could tie the Chillblaines brothers to the damage done at camp."

Pastor Randy hesitated for a moment, feeling a bit guilty. "Yeah, Sheriff, I do believe I do have some information. I know I should have gone to you first, but I consented to Buddy sneaking over to the Chillblaines's place to look for the device or devices that made the Bigfoot tracks in the dirt. I'm largely responsible for almost getting Buddy killed."

"You're right, Pastor. You should have contacted me first. But at least we have the situation under control. So, you believe that the tracks we saw around the buildings were also done by the Chillblaines brothers?"

"That's right, Sheriff."

"Well now that is quite interesting. I have a written statement from Hector saying that both brothers were responsible for the wreckage. But Hector never mentioned anything about making those tracks. Why do you believe the brothers made them?"

"Actually, this isn't the first time that Buddy was at the Chillblaines's place," Pastor Randy confessed. "Both he and his sister made a little trip over there and were almost caught a few days ago."

"Now that's beginning to make sense, Sheriff Greene spoke as if a light bulb had gone on in his head. "The Chillblaines came to the station in Northridge and complained that a couple of people had been seen exiting their house."

"Okay, while the two campers were in the basement, they saw a gorilla suit hanging up. Sheriff, do you remember those Bigfoot-sighting reports that have been going around?"

"Yeah."

"Well, the Chambers kids believe that those sightings were based on the Chillblaines brothers dressing the gorilla costume upon a type of robot and then sending it out to scare the campers. You know they have the money to do such a thing. To make a long story short, Buddy put two and two together and figured that the Bigfoot tracks were also coming from the Chillblaines. That is why Buddy was looking for the track-makers. He thought that if the irregularities in the tracks could be matched to similar markings on the foot devices, he would have proof that Horace and Hector were the ones behind the whole shebang. We suspect that the brothers are trying to scare away the campers so that they won't come back to Camp Musky."

"Now things are really beginning to make sense," Sheriff Greene said knowingly. "Hector in his interrogation told me that Horace wanted to silence Buddy for that very reason. Thanks for the info, Pastor." Sheriff Greene folded his cell phone and put it into his pocket.

*****

After obtaining a search warrant to search the Chillblaines's basement, Sheriff Greene drove up to their mansion. He found the basement door, as the brothers had left it, unlocked.

He searched every inch of the basement but didn't find the track makers or a gorilla suit. "I wonder if they took them upstairs," he mused out loud.

Sheriff Greene knew that his search warrant didn't allow him to search upstairs, but he figured that this was a special case, and so he justified his decision to do so.

Without disturbing any of the house's contents, he searched every room in the mansion. In fact, he searched each room twice, but still, he could find no track makers. Finally, he left the building and drove back to Northridge.

*****

Soon after Pastor Randy had spoken to Sheriff Greene over the phone, he received another call. This time, it was from Dave Chambers.

"Pastor Randy, Jack Mason told me this morning in the Northridge Hospital that he thinks it's possible that a demonic force crashed the helicopter he was flying. With all the bad things happening around here, I wonder if he is correct. Maybe we should have a prayer meeting scheduled at camp. If you do have such a meeting. I'd like to attend."

"That's a good idea," the youth pastor confirmed. "We could have one this evening after you are done with work. Say, around six o'clock?"

"Sounds good," Dave replied. "I'll be there."

*****

Stanley couldn't know that the search and rescue team had come within a quarter mile of him that very morning. The men, who had called out to him until they were hoarse, had gone by him in relative silence. Some had used whistles, but after prolonged blowing, the shrillness of these had worked greatly upon the searchers' nerves, and they had stopped blowing them.

He was out in the blackberry patch getting lunch. Stanley had found a few other food sources including a wild apple tree, but most of his nourishment came from the blackberries. This diet was a little monotonous, but he was thankful for something to eat.

He carefully wedged his way through the berry patch so as not to get scratched on the thorns. Suddenly he heard a crashing noise about one hundred feet in front of him. Hoping the noise came from a rescuer, he called out.

Everything went silent.

Stanley was bewildered. What had caused the thrashing in the bushes? He didn't have long to find out.

A *huff* brought his attention to the biggest black bear he had ever seen, rising up on its two hind legs.

The bear sniffed in the direction of Stanley. It was extremely concerned for its two cubs which were hidden by the berry bushes. Stanley remained frozen. With a growl, the she bear crashed through the berry patch toward him.

Now Stanley's adrenaline took over, and he sprinted for his life. He thought of jumping into the windfall, but the bear could easily tear into that.

Where could he go?

To his right, Stanley noticed a partially hollowed-out tree that he hadn't remembered seeing before. He headed for it. A crack in the dead tree extended the length of the trunk. Somehow with all of his strength, he forced himself into the crack.

The bear came to a sliding halt as it slammed into the tree. It growled ferociously. Its claws ripped into the rotten bark. But try as she might, the bear could not extend its paws far enough into the tree to reach him.

Soon the two cubs came ambling up to their mother. She sniffed at them, making sure that they were all right. Then with a growl, she led the cubs away into the forest.

Stanley was shaking both from fatigue and from fright. He waited about a half hour before even trying to exit the tree.

Slowly he pushed his left arm through the crack in the tree, Next, he tried with great effort to force his body through this aperture. It wouldn't go through. He tried again and again, getting no better results. Finally, with a rising sense of panic, Stanley realized he couldn't get out of the tree. He must have relied upon his adrenaline and fear of the bear to get in. But now, try as he might, he couldn't get out. The only thing to do was to wait inside the tree trunk for someone to rescue him. At least he could sit down inside the tree even if his knees were bent straight up to his chin.

*****

Horace Chillblaines was not talking on the recommendation of his lawyer. Every time the sheriff questioned him; he just pled the Fifth Amendment. Sheriff Greene was growing impatient with him, but of course, he didn't want to show it.

"So, Horace, we can do this the hard way or the easy way," he said nonchalantly to the elderly man, staring him in the eye. "As you know, I've got Hector's sworn statement confessing everything you two did. And he is ready to testify about the kidnapping and of the Chambers boy attempted murder too. Why don't you now just confess to all of this before it goes to trial? We could work out a deal for a lesser charge against you and the penalty could be reduced. What do you say?"

Horace pled the Fifth.

*****

The search and rescue team dragged themselves wearily back to the camp just as Dave Chambers pulled up to the camp's main meeting hall at six o'clock. By the looks on the men's faces, Dave knew instantly that they hadn't found Stanley.

"No results from the search today?" he questioned the team leader. The man glanced at Dave and shook his head.

Pastor Randy came out of the meeting hall's front door followed by Bud and Cally. "Hi, Dave," the youth pastor called out as the Chambers kids hugged their dad. "Well now, let's all go inside for our prayer meeting," Pastor Randy invited. "Your search and rescue folks are welcome to come and join us."

Some did.

When they had gone inside the meeting hall, Pastor Randy began the prayer service. Some sat in chairs, others kneeled down, and others stood in reverent positions. Each one had his or her turn to pray, and almost everyone took advantage of the opportunity. It was indeed a glorious and blessed time.

*****

Darkness began to settle over the land, and Stanley realized that he was about to spend the night in this tree trunk, cramped and hungry. Not only that, but his full bladder was calling for relief. He was already stiff from being in here for hours. "Lord, I need Your help to get out of here and to get back to camp," he prayed.

Suddenly a light brighter than the moon, brighter than the sun, burst upon the darkness. He shielded his eyes from the brilliance, which shined in through the split in the tree's trunk. A cracking sound entered his ears, and then the tree trunk exploded, sending pieces of wood outward in all directions.

Stanley found himself sitting outside of his onetime prison, and yet he was in the very place he had been all afternoon and evening.

"What just happened?" he muttered aloud.

Had someone fired off a stick of dynamite on the tree trunk? That was unlikely, for he was unscathed. Dynamite would also have blown him to "smithereens" along with the wood. He reflected back to the cracking sound just before the tree trunk had exploded. It had sounded like a giant ripped the trunk apart with his bare hands.

"Could it have been an angel?" he asked incredulously. "That must be the answer. Thank You, Lord!" Stanley yelled to the heavens.

*****

During the prayer meeting, Pastor Randy and the others thought they heard the sound of thunder. They paused and looked out the windows. To their astonishment, they saw a brilliant light for several moments far out in the distance. Then it vanished.

"Are we having a rainstorm this evening?" Cally asked Pastor Randy.

"No, dear, not tonight. The sky is clear, and you can see the stars."

"What was that light then?" Buddy inquired.

"I believe that light shows us the way to where Stanley is," Pastor Randy said with a satisfied smile upon his face.

*****

Two glowing eyes peered intently at Stanley from the edge of the forest as he lay sleeping peacefully in the windfall. The creature was huge, and it emitted a foul-smelling odor from its great bulk. It growled a deep, guttural sound from its throat as it impatiently waited for a chance to attack the boy.

But there was no chance for it to attack. A ring of heavenly angels, their swords drawn, surrounded the peacefully sleeping boy. But Stanley could not have seen them even if he had been awake.

The creature in great frustration growled once again and then turned and vanished into the night's air.

*****

The next morning, as soon as it was light enough to see, Pastor Randy and Pete Foster dressed and without showering or shaving began their quest to find Stanley. Dave Chambers elected to stay with the campers.

The two hopeful rescuers stuffed their pockets with granola bars and filled their canteens with cool refreshing water. Pastor Randy took a compass, reading on the spot where they had seen the light the evening before. Then the two set out on that compass reading with high hopes of finding the Foster boy.

*****

Horace Chillblaines knew that he was in deep trouble. If his idiot brother hadn't "blabbed" his guts to the sheriff, then everything might be just fine. He had had last night to think things out and he knew that if his case went before a judge and jury, he wouldn't have much of a chance. He thought about confessing his crimes to the sheriff for a reduced sentence, but even that didn't appeal to him very much. No, sir, at his age, even a reduced sentence might cause him to spend the rest of his life in prison. For the first time in many years, Horace Chillblaines was feeling fear.

He called his lawyer to ask his advice on what he should do. Horace didn't have many options. He could face a judge and jury, he could possibly plead to a lesser crime with a reduced sentence, or hmmm... Perhaps he could get the Chambers boy to drop the charges. Horace told his lawyer that he wanted him to call Camp Musky and "reason" with Buddy.

*****

Stanley was out in the blackberry patch getting his buffet lunch when he heard the thrashing in the bushes about fifty yards away. At first, he thought that the black bear and its cubs were back, and a bolt of fear burst through him. However, to his relief, as he turned toward the thrashing noise, he saw the familiar forms of his dad and Pastor Randy.

The three shouted greetings simultaneously and rushed together to embrace each other.

"Stanley! Oh, how good it is to see you, son!" Mr. Foster exclaimed. "Are you all right?"

"Yes, Dad, I'm fine. As you can see, I have all I need to eat. And I've been sleeping in a five-star hotel." He pointed to the blackberry patch and the windfall.

The trio laughed at Stanley's remarks, feeling joyous that everything was well with him.

After several more minutes of hugs and reassurances, Stanley, his dad, and Pastor Randy headed back to camp.

*****

The phone rang at Camp Musky, and Dave Chambers answered it. The voice on the other end was abrupt and business-like.

"This is George Bullard, Horace Chillblaines's attorney. With whom am I speaking, please?"

"Uh, my name is Dave Chambers," Dave spoke with suspicion.

"Are you Buddy Chambers's dad?"

"Yes. What is this call about anyway?" Dave still remained suspicious.

"Well, I'd like to speak to your son Buddy, if I may."

"What do you want to speak to him about?" Dave's suspicion reached a peak at this point.

"That would be a private conversation between him and me."

"You know that he's a minor, don't you? At least you should know that, Mr. Bullard. Anything you have to say to him, you need to speak to me about first."

George Bullard paused for a few moments. "All right, Mr. Chambers. Horace wanted Buddy to drop the charges against him."

"Horace wanted what?" Dave asked incredulously.

"He wanted Buddy to drop the charges against him," the lawyer repeated. "You know, Mr. Chambers, it might be a good idea for you folks if he did. It could save everyone an embarrassingly long, drawn out court trial. Not to mention the expense of it."

"Well, it sounds like Horace is desperate and that he just wants to save his face!" Dave spoke indignantly and a little stronger than he usually did. "Drop charges against that murderin' weasel? Not on your life, Bullard!"

"Consider this, Mr. Chambers. Horace Chillblaines has millions of dollars. He can afford a long trial if need be. And he can afford the best legal defense that there is!" Bullard was arrogantly referring to himself by that last comment.

"He can't buy himself out of this case!" Dave said emphatically. He was about to slam the phone onto its receiver when George Bullard made a final comment. "At least discuss the situation with your son. He's the one that this case will really affect."

"That I will do, Mr. Bullard. That I will do!"

*****

It was late in the afternoon when Pastor Randy, Stanley, and his dad made their way back to the camp. Everyone was excited, joyous, and full of questions about what had happened to Stanley all at the same time.

Stanley felt somewhat like a celebrity and answered the questions directly and as simply as possible. At times, he almost sounded nonchalant at the plights he had been in.

"Oh, I wasn't scared most of the time," Stanley replied to one of Clarence's questions. "I did almost get attacked by a bear though."

Clarence's eyes nearly bugged out of his head.

"And an angel blew apart a tree trunk I was stuck in."

"Wow," the campers echoed together.

Stanley seemed to take on heroic proportions to his peers.

Chapter 9

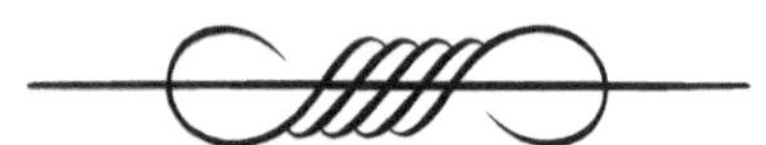

Dave Chambers discussed the issue with his son and Cally of dropping the charges against Horace Chillblaines.

"What do you think I should do, Dad?" Buddy inquired earnestly.

"It's really your decision, Bud," his father said thoughtfully. "But whatever you decide, don't let the cost of the case sway you. We'll manage somehow."

"Well, I believe that Horace shouldn't just get away, scot-free," Buddy said, feeling a strong sense of justice. "He needs to learn that he can't do anything he wants to and then suffer no consequences."

"Good for you, Buddy," his father encouraged him.

The three discussed every aspect of the situation of which they could think. Then they came up with a plan.

*****

Stanley ate a hearty supper that evening. He had lost several pounds while out in the wilds and now felt better than he had in his life. He decided to go to his cabin early and get some well-needed rest.

*****

Buddy and Cally went to their respective cabins for the night. Both of them slept fitfully and were up early the next morning. They found Dad already in the cafeteria, and the three ate breakfast together.

"This morning, we'll break the news to Horace and his attorney," Dave Chambers said to his children with a grim look. "It'll be up to him whether he accepts the terms of the plan."

After finishing their meal and praying, the three got into Mr. Chambers's vehicle and made the trip to Northridge.

As the Chambers family entered the county jail, they saw that George Bullard was already in the office section working on some forms. He looked up with a start.

"Well, well, if it isn't Buddy Chambers and his clan, I suppose. What have you decided Buddy? Are you going to freely drop the charges against Horace?"

"Not exactly, sir," the youth replied. "I've come to make a deal with Horace if he'll negotiate."

"What's the deal, son?" Bullard asked anxiously.

"Well," Buddy replied hesitantly. He glanced over at his dad who was smiling at him. "I'll drop all charges against Horace on one and only one condition. I'll do it if he will sign another twenty-year contract to keep Camp Musky open, and if he'll stop harassing all campers and pay for the damages done."

George Bullard nodded slowly. "I see. I'll bring your deal to Horace and see if he'll accept the terms."

Bullard went to Horace's cell and dropped the deal on him. Horace fussed and fumed for a while but saw nothing else he could do but accept the terms. Reluctantly he agreed and signed papers to that intent.

When the Chambers family found out the good news, they let out a loud "whoopie."

*****

Back at Camp Musky, the Chambers family joined the other campers in cleaning up the broken glass and other debris on the campgrounds. Today was the last day of camp, and they wanted things to look as good as possible for the closing church service this evening.

The day passed swiftly, and the time finally came for the service to begin. As the campers and staff were entering the chapel, Buddy and Cally noticed a big black limousine pulled up into the camp's parking lot. To their astonishment, when the door of the vehicle opened, out stepped Hector Chillblaines, dressed in a dark suit. He, of course, had been released from jail along with Horace earlier in the day. But Horace was not with him now.

"Hello, children," Hector spoke to Buddy and Cally in a pleasant voice. Before the two could answer him, he added quickly, "I've come this evening to apologize for everything my brother and I have done."

The Chambers siblings smiled at him and allowed him to enter the chapel before them. When he found a place to sit down on one of the benches, the two sat beside him.

After everyone was seated, Pastor Randy greeted them from the pulpit, giving special attention to Hector. They sang several choruses and then had a special time of prayer. Soon Pastor Randy started giving his last message for this year to the assembled group. His eyes filled with tears as he affectionately talked heart-to-heart with everyone, even thanking Hector for keeping the camp open in the years to come. He spoke from several passages of the Bible, and in his conclusion, he gave an invitation for anyone here to come forward to the front of the chapel to receive Christ as Lord and Savior.

Buddy and Cally went forward to recommit their lives to the Lord. Stanley went forward to show publicly that he was now trusting in Christ, and to everyone's surprise, Hector Chillblaines got up from his bench and went forward to receive Christ for the first time. Others did too.

After hugging Pastor Randy, Stanley, and all the others said "goodbye." Buddy and Cally left Camp Musky with their dad for another year. Since it was not too late in the evening, they decided to stop in Northridge to say hi to mom before going home.

As the Chambers's vehicle was departing down the long driveway of Camp Musky, a large splash on Moose Lake was glimpsed by the three as the truck's headlights reflected upon the spray of the lake's waters. It seemed to them almost like a farewell tribute.

"You don't think that the big musky was saying goodbye, do you?" Buddy asked in amazement.

"Stranger things have happened," Dad said with a twinkle in his eyes.

"You said that right," Cally remarked with a smile.

The truck exited the long driveway, and Dave turned right onto Route 27, heading for the town of Moose Lake and ultimately for Northridge.

They were all singing choruses when they entered the Northridge Hospital parking lot. Visiting hours would be over in a half hour, so the trio hurried to make it to Linda's room.

She was still awake when her family members entered the room. Dave had not called ahead so as not to disturb her if she was asleep. Linda was delighted to see them and expressed her pleasure verbally.

The four chatted for a time, catching up on some of the events of the past few days. Finally, Dave asked his wife about the situation which had been the cause for her being here at the hospital for Buddy and Cally's sake.

"What do you think you hit with the SUV, sending you to Northridge, honey?"

Linda thought for a moment. "I'm really not sure," she said. Her mind went back to the moment of that event. "It was something huge and black. I thought later that it might have been a bear, but now I just don't know."

"You think that it might have been a Bigfoot?" Cally inquired. The others grinned at her question.

"I've never believed in Bigfoot, dear," Linda spoke to her daughter. "I don't think that they even exist."

"Well, whatever you hit, we're just thankful that you're all right," Dave said gratefully.

"Yes," Linda said. "The doctor thinks I'll be out of the hospital in a day or two."

A nurse entered the room and told them that visiting time would be over in a couple of minutes. They then kissed Linda goodnight, had a little prayer, and left for home.

On the way, the three got cold chills as they came to the place where Linda had had her accident. They could still see the tire marks on the road where the SUV had skidded.

Later that evening, they turned onto their own driveway and pulled into the garage. How wonderful it felt to be home.

*****

Cally didn't know it at the time, but one day she would marry Stanley Foster. Stanley would eventually own a chain of five-star hotels called the Windfall.

Buddy would become a pastor and would one day take Pastor Randy's place as director of Camp Musky.

For the rest of his life, Hector helped Camp Musky in any way he could, even donating large sums of money to keep it running.